The Goodbye Family
and the Great Mountain

by

Lorin Morgan-Richards
Author and Illustrator

Foreword by Richard-Lael Lillard
Edited by Jessica Rose Felix

To Valerie, Berlin and Karen, with thanks

ISBN: 9781733287951
A Raven Above Press
Copyright 2020
Studio City, CA
www.lorinrichards.com

Table of Contents

I. These Remains	13
II. The Goodbye Family	19
III. Rufus Ain't Right	29
IV. A Cure for All	39
V. Mistaken Heir	47
VI. Otis in Nicklesworth	59
VII. The Plan	75
VIII. The Old Cemetery	83
IX. Entering Nothom	93
X. On the Trail	105
XI. Descent	109
XII. A Tourist Trap	121
XIII. Thorne Recollects	131
XIV. Bridge of Sighs	135
XV. More Disappointment	143
XVI. The Antiquarium Library	153
XVII. Fleck	159
XVIII. Movin' on Up	171
XIX. The Mission	175
XX. Disaster Pastor	181
XXI. Cata-Chthonic	185
XXII. Pyridine's Remorse	203
XXIII. Feeling Scrappy	207
XXIV. A Nose for Rain	211
XXV. The Disturbed	219
XXVI. Posy Palace	227
XXVII. The Big Chill	235
XXVIII. In a Pickle	245

Foreword
by Richard-Lael Lillard

Say hello to the Goodbyes. This is a heartwarming story of magic, mystery, and fantasy, but most of all, adventure.

I am a dreamer, and I have had such spectacular journeys through the realms of slumber. Years and years ago, I got into the habit of sharing my dreams on social media. Where some people have tried to give amateur interpretations to my dreams, others have contented themselves with the thought that the dreams are mere flights of fancy. Others still have made comments inquiring about my diet, saying, "perhaps it is a bit of undigested beef, blot of mustard, crumb of cheese, or fragment of an underdone potato." However...It was through these posts, that I began to notice one friend in particular, who stood out as a beguiling beacon in the darkness. This friend would find direct correlations between my dreams and long ago historical facts, frequently sharing these findings with me. He has an excellent gift for research and an intuitive understanding of times long past.

I have long admired the artistry and talent of Lorin Morgan-Richards. He paints a darkly colorful world. A world that is inhabited by richly detailed characters, whose interwoven stories remind of the magic of Oz, the visual stylings of Roald Dahl, with the perfect mixture of the macabre and quirkiness of Charles

Addams.

One of my fondest memories as a child was going to the library. Reading expanded my mind, lifted my spirit, and sparked creativity. Yes, we can read via technology, but there is no greater feeling than that of a physical book. The feel of the pages on my fingertips, the weight of the book, and the smell of the ink is nothing less than magic. Escape the chaos of the modern world, and be inspired by the one inhabited by the Goodbye Family. In this immersive story, you will encounter a menagerie of eccentric characters, all of whom you will find endearingly charming. With his formidable knowledge of delightfully obscure Victoriana, Lorin Morgan-Richards adds a richness and a depth unheard of by his contemporaries.

The author is a fount of esoteric wisdom, which is evident in this modern-day classic. My hope for you, dear reader, is that you enjoy this masterpiece until the book is at the point of physical disintegration, and the pages fall out, so you need to carry them around in a plastic bag sealed with a rubber band.

Introduction

The Great Purple Mountain divided the land into four climates: fall weather in the east, arid summer desert in the south, spring warmth in the west, and winter tundra in the north. The Goodbye family, along with miners, farmers, and capitalists, inhabited areas east of the Great Mountain after the war between the Boorish and the Tried. Baron Von Nickle, a Boorish capitalist who started the war to seize land and resources, sent his army west over the grassland, destroying the homes of the villagers as he went. This once diverse area where animals roamed free and trees thrived fast became depleted of its natural resources as the greedy Baron looked for more ways to live opulently. To the west of the Great Mountain, and most impassable by all, were thought to be rivers running through luscious purple leaf forests. The lesser known northern quadrant howled with chilly winds, where the climate was icy cold. From the south, the southern winds blew hot and dry, an area expected to be a vast desert.

Very few had ever traversed all four regions and lived to share their knowledge of the interconnectedness of all the lands. Most of those that saw all four lost their lives in the war against the Baron. One, however, did not partake in the fighting as he believed in harmony with Nature and the spirit realm. He kept his knowledge secret from the public, fearful of what it could do in the wrong hands. But as time passed, he could see his granddaughter, Me'ma, showing extraordinary gifts. The child was the only one to whom he bestowed his wisdom of the spirit world and the purple leaf tree. In Sunken Creek, the grandfather spent many hours teaching the traditional ways to the child using the purple leaf tree as the instrument of learning.

The Baron sent his army, led by Frank Thorne, into Sunken Creek clearing the land of the villagers and forcing them to work in his mine. Me'ma was able to escape but was displaced from her grandfather. The little girl discovered allies along her journey, helping her to overcome her fears, and focus on the traditions her grandfather had taught her to free her people from the evil tyrant.

The Baron's weakness was in his greed for gold. But it was not the only venture he had a stake. Many years before the war, his teenage son discovered oil by striking a well in what was their first attempt at mining. The son was raised by his mother, and unlike his father, wanted to help people. One night he met a strange prophet named Zenwick, who inspected the oil and convinced him it had healing properties. The son asked for his father's help in getting this healing miracle to those who needed it most. But the Baron laughed at the idea of gifting their valuable find to commoners. Soon the scientific community condemned the oil as a fraud. The Baron's wealthy peers ridiculed the son, and the son was cast out of his father's life.

Broken and in despair, the son, took to drinking the remaining bottles of his oil tonic. After several nights of this, he collapsed at the doorstep of the prophet Zenwick. When the son awakened the following morning, he was not the same person. His mind had been emptied. Zenwick said a foreign presence had taken over the young man's body, guiding him with sinister intent. Zenwick, who was equally corrupt, demanded a meeting with the Baron to show the effects of the tonic on his estranged son. The tonic was a miracle potion indeed; instead of healing whoever drank it, it reduced them to a state of living death. In this, the Baron saw great opportunities.

At the outbreak of the war, Zenwick and his son demonstrated the tonic's lasting power on the Baron's army. Even the most hardened soldiers went into a deep sleep and re-awoke with an evil vigor to fight and win. It enhanced not only the soldier's inability to feel pain but also their viciousness to succeed. Zenwick ordered the Baron to monetize their oil business or else. The Baron hesitantly ceded, and Zenwick moved to a remote area in the south of the Great Mountain to build his empire. The Baron now had the tonic to control his new army, and he set his sights on the world.

Underneath the Great Mountain, Zenwick's drilling was wreaking havoc. The moles, snakes, lizards, and even underground fish suffered as their delicate ecosystem was destroyed. Most deeply disturbed were the Goodbyes, for whom this story is named, and the underworld from which the oil expelled.

Thorne was a product of both worlds, having succumbed to death only to be restored to life by a foreign presence within the tonic.

Chapter I. These Remains

The shrill caw of crows flying off awoke the dead body of Frank Thorne. He was hanging off a cliff. The remains of his army were not in any way gruesome or sad, as they appeared to be more like broken toy soldiers than human. Thorne and his ex-band were not typical soldiers. They felt very little pain, and instead of blood in their veins, they had bugs tunneling inside their mummified cavities. Thorne's men had died years ago as outlaws, thieves, and cutthroats that had been eternally enslaved to build the Baron's army. No one knew how they came back to life. It was a mystery no one dared investigate. Thorne's skin was tight and pale blue color, and his eyes and lips bulged from an equally swollen head. His ears and nose were decaying as his bony joints sharply contrasted in his crusty clothes that gave off a horrible stench of sulfur.

Thorne's head churned with a montage of his last memories; Baron Von Nickle plummeting at high speed into the river of the Great Mountain. It was not until an hour had passed that Thorne realized he was not so much in a bad dream but at the tail end of a significant defeat by Me'ma, the Indigenous child from Sunken Creek. He wrestled a wolf and was flung off the cliff like a ragdoll. Luckily, his whip was the first to fall as it snagged on a root sticking out from the rocks. Thorne was snared by the tangled whip saving his life. His right foot was strangulated at the ankle, so to an outside observer, it might appear he was doing upside down jumping jacks.

Gathering his wits, the outlaw panned the devastation around him. His bent rifle was stuck in the ground with his hat beside it. The camp where so many struck it rich, laid trampled and deserted. Thorne could see the river littered with debris from the turned over mining camp, and further in the distance, he saw the steamboat fading back east towards the town of Nicklesworth. Crows flew down from the mountain peak cheerily picking at the decomposing remnants of the camp. He could hear them speak and thought it was at first a delusion of his fall. "That looks perfect for my nest," one cawed, taking a pair of overalls into its beak. "The king will be pleased with these treasures," another curiously said digging into a backpack. A rather small bird honed in on Thorne's hat, landing several feet from the outlaw. Thorne flailed his body, trying to scare away the crow but watched helplessly as the bird flew off with its heist.

Thorne's temper erupted. "Dang gum junk rustling, thieving coyote howling cauliflower cawing fruit flies!" He yelled, making very little sense and stirring with so much emotion, he started to look like a giant beaten piñata. The last of his favorite sugar cubes fell from his pockets to the ground below. "Gosh dang picket poppers!" He exclaimed, meaning to say pick-pockets, but most everything was coming out upside down. He repeatedly cursed and swung at the crows until all at once, his back smacked against the rocks, loosening him from the whip and finally scaring the birds off with the loud noise when he fell.

SMACK!

Thorne dropped a short distance down to the trail below and lifted to his knees. His injured ankle could not support his weight. It did not hurt so much as deterred him. Nearby laid his rifle, now bent in the shape of a shepherd's crook from the accident. The angry man crawled to the gun and was about to throw it in frustration when he realized the rifle could be used as a cane. He placed his weight on the firearm and lifted himself up. Thorne was already a crooked man, so it was by no intentional design he now had a body to suit him. Thorne dug into his pockets for any remaining sugar cubes but found only a few taunting granules. So he licked his fingers and yelled at the birds: "Tell me, where is the Baron!?" The crows stared bleakly at him quite aware of his escaped presence.

Thorne searched through the wreckage for his master. He looked under ripped canvas, broken wagons, and fallen rocks. But the desperate man only found broken pieces of the camp and a few scattered limbs of his accomplices that fell from the cliff.

Thorne followed the river east and noticed a derby hat floating alongside the riverbank. He hobbled to the water and fished out the hat using the crook of his bent rifle. "Ah, what gem have I found." The outlaw could see the hat made of black beaver was crushed on one side and connected most unkindly to three twisted rattail hair strands that belonged to the Baron. The vile man looked into the river in finality where he thought he spotted a glimmer of gold from the depths. The faint voice of the Baron was heard in the back of his mind: *"Finish my bidding."*

Thorne raised his voice in rage. "You lost it all Baron. All you thought about was the gold that buried you." It was then for a moment; he thought he could hear his heartbeat. But he knew he had none. The pounding beat faded as a drum echoed off the canyon wall from the other side of the Great Mountain where unbeknownst to him Me'ma and her villagers celebrated their freedom. In anger, Thorne ripped the strands of hair stuck to the Baron's hat and threw them into the dirt. He raised his derby hat pointedly at a crow, "I will end this," he said placing the hat on his head and hobbling with his cane back to Nicklesworth. He shooed away the crows, knowing no other would dare to cross him. No one would be able to challenge him. No one would stand in his way. Only a fool, would do so.

Chapter II. The Goodbye Family

Mr. Otis Goodbye took special care of driving the town's hearse. His job was routinely inspecting his dearly departed to look their best, and delivering them to their final destination. His daughter, Orphie, liked to ride beside her father, while his wife, Pyridine, stayed in the back keeping the casket and tools from making a terrible racket.

The Goodbye Family lived in a community called Slug, named for Abraham Slug who emigrated from a place called Hole with his family on the merchant ship Sea Slug. Mr. Slug was contracted to build the nearby town of Nicklesworth by the ruthless tycoon Baron Von Nickle and only given a few leaves to which he said he did not "lichen." Mr. Slug is also responsible for the Slime Trail that leads into town.

The frontier times and growing capitalism was ripe with superstitions and funerary customs, all of which made the Goodbyes minor celebrities in their area. The Goodbye Family's residence was constructed from the remains of a giant Montezuma cypress tree, the oldest and largest in the land.

Their original home was burned during the war and left the family to move into the nearby tree. It too, along with other structures in Slug sustained damage from the fighting, but due to its enormous size and veins on the outermost layers, survived and created a liveable habitat for the Goodbyes.

Though they felt comfortable in their unusual tree, they had to pay rent on it. The Baron claimed to own everything; buildings, boats, and all the land's resources, including the rivers, rocks, and trees and expected people to pay their share for its use.

The house fire impacted the family in many ways, and they lost many rare specimens, including an insect broach called the Chromus Humbug that Otis gave to his wife when they were engaged to be married.

The Chromus Humbug was a rare and most beautiful turquoise shelled insect that stayed semi-dormant eating small pesky insects around its host as it clung to fabric without the need for a pin or clasp. The Chromus Humbug had the unique ability to release a pungent toxin from its abdomen in self-defense. However, injuring it could also trigger it to release its foul stench on the poor soul who breathed it. A most deadly and desired accessory for Pyridine, but scarce indeed.

When they first moved into their tree house, it was a burnt hollow of ringed layers which they cherished. Otis was an experienced carpenter from his work with caskets and thoughtfully connected the levels of their house with staircases, shelves, and other necessities. They made their makeshift home more unusual, filling it in with bizarre and macabre artifacts from around the land.

Otis also had an exceptional ability to smell odors in the air, and it just so happened that when Mrs. Everyday across town expired, it called to his attention.

Otis flipped the reins of Midnight, their horse, and blew the sound of a raspberry to which the horse perferred over kissing noises, leading the carriage away from their home.

"Father, who are we picking up this evening?" asked the child.

Otis lifted his nose in the air to smell the direction of demise.

"Meriweather Everyday," he said confidently, "the wife of a scientist just down the road."

Pyridine overheard the conversation through a small carriage window. "I never knew Mrs. Everydays husband was a scientist. What did he specialize in?"

"I haven't a clue. Perhaps stargazing? In any case, our old night watchman had to kick him out of the cemetery a few times," said Otis. "Hopefully, we will meet him today, P."

(Otis was in the habit of calling his wife "P," while Pyridine was in the habit of calling her husband "Poo," for altogether different reasons.)

Beside her father, Orphie twirled around a second-hand spade. She had incredible strength, and her parents thought because of this, she was ready to apprentice as a gravedigger. She was between six and seven, and her hair was a grown out bob of distressed blonde. The child enjoyed wearing her Grandmother Yeast's clothes, who was quite short herself. She always wore her shoes backward, and all her clothes had been played in roughly or were so very itchy that Pyridine had to patch and resew fabric over the worst offenders, leaving her dress in a variety of lace and brown cloth.

Orphie had an older brother named Kepla, but he was a complete mystery around the house. While mostly in hiding, the parents went on mentioning him just as if he was present. In fact, they celebrated his birthday in December and said his age was ten years older than Otis and Pyridine, which made it even that much more bizarre. Luckily Orphie still could not count that high to question it.

Pyridine, the matriarch, mortician, and witch of the house had flowing locks of lavender pulled into a tight braid that hung below her waist. The hair used to drag behind her on the ground, but she had recently cut it to provide a nest for her pet trocar, an enchanted embalming rod.

The trocar was a foot and a half long and used interchangeably for her mortuary duties (letting out gas and bloating), and as a crop to playfully correct Otis's disposition. The handle worked nicely in puffing up her shoulder pads, and the needle could tighten screws on a casket. Not to mention, she found it handy to take rough measurements. Most importantly, outside of its functionality, as a witch, she used this rod to fly. She once used brooms, but these were *harry* and prone to fall apart. It was also considered merely for beginners. Likewise, she had enchanted an umbrella before the invention of the embalming rod, but an umbrella was unreliable, malfunctioning, and *poppin'* up at the worst moments. Besides, she thought, who carries an umbrella when a hardy steel embalming rod was both practical, stylish and neatly fit into a purse?

Pyridine was an expert in alchemy and knew that it took just a few drops of Blister Beetle sweat to bring a chair or table to life. Luckily, Orphie only had a chance to try it on her father's hat and mother's embalming rod. Both now could fly short distances.

Pyridine's uniform was a tight dress of dark purple, and she always carried her magic trocar (when it was not flying), and a set of golden shears and crooked needles inside her large black mortician's bag.

Otis usually dressed in a brown tailcoat and matching stovepipe top hat with a crow's feather attached. The feather of course for short distance flight. He had slicked brown hair that appeared black from bear fat and a thin handlebar mustache and goatee he groomed on his face. His bowtie was a dirty shade of blue or orange depending on his mood. That is, a mood changing bowtie. In his sleeve, Otis had a soiled handkerchief from his wife, a bug in his boot from his unaccountable son, a stain on his shirt from his daughter and nibbled cuffs from his horse. He carried in his pockets several keys and carpenter tools and making his situation even more cumbersome, these pockets were inside other pockets and quite challenging to find in a flash. One of the pockets he reserved for his horse Midnight, where he stuck several pickles. Midnight loved to eat anything pickled. Needless to say, he smelled of vinegar which Pyridine didn't mind having to work with so many various chemicals herself.

The carriage continued down the road and seeing his daughter look bored, Otis asked, "Would you like to hear a story to pass the time?"

Orphie's eyes widened. "I would," she answered. "You owe me the ending to the cattle poacher Not-Home?"
"You mean Mr. Nothom," Otis recalled, making the double raspberry noise and flopping the reins of the horse to trot.

Orphie's favorite story was about a legendary cattle poacher named Walter Nothom, a giant among men who branded himself with the distinct marks of every ranch he poached. He could walk through tornados with a whole flock of sheep in his arms and corralled cattle with a simple whoosh of his gargantuan hands. There was always a wealth of lore surrounding Nothom. Otis pondered where to begin this time.

"There was branding on his left shoulder of a bull from the McKann's Ranch..."

"No, no," Pyridine scolded through the window. "I think you better wait a few years' before you tell her that one."

"Right then," Otis agreed. "On the other side of his body he had branded himself with the sign of the McCant's Ranch..."

"McCant's?" Orphie interrupted.

"Yes, that's right. McCant was a conjoined twin, and only one of Old Man McCant's heads was male you see, and they had some sheep."

"We're here!" Pyridine shouted, as the carriage and the story abruptly stopped. Orphie stepped down to find a pink mailbox at the end of a driveway with the name "Everyday," brushed happily across it.

Otis gasped aloud at the color. "It's worse than I thought, they're completely deranged!"

The Everyday Estate was unaffected by the war and painted

in a lime green pastel and gated all around with a bubblegum pink picket fence to match the mailbox. Several wooden roosters sunbathed in the garden with the statement "Peace on Earth."

"Doesn't Slug have restrictions for this kind of house?" Orphie asked with a shrug. Otis stepped off the carriage and joined his daughter. He then pulled out a pickle from his pocket and fed it to their horse, tying her to the fence. Pyridine exited the wagon and stretched herself out one appendage at a time releasing a satisfying Snap, Crack. Pop from every joint. "Ah, that feels better."

"Would you hand me my medicine bag?" Otis asked his wife. "This is a more dire case than I thought."

"Why do you say that, father?"

"The Everydays may be suffering from Normalitis," Otis frowned. A terribly contagious disease that causes one to lose their discernment. It was mentioned in the journal of Morbid Science just last week."

"Say it isn't so!" Pyridine said bleakly, covering her child's ears, "sounds like some sort of brain worm."

Chapter III. Rufus Ain't Right

Orphie hoisted the casket over her head and dragged it to the Everydays front door. The girl could carry ten times her weight. Her parents reasoned she had the recessive genes of her father's Great grandfather, King Konzo, a circus strongman who fell in love with a sea banshee named Queen Bacillus. His last words were:

I fell for her eyes
I fell for her wail
I fell for her disguise
I tripped over her tail.

Pyridine and Otis prepped their tools and braced themselves for what horrors awaited.

They tip-toed through a garden blooming with impatiens so fragrant it gave Otis a nosebleed.

"You should really get that checked out," said Pyridine. Otis stuffed a handkerchief in his nostril to quell the gushing red and proceeded with his family to the doorstep, where they waited by a doormat with the words, 'Everyday Family' spelled out in colorful stones.

Pyridine curiously peeked inside the front window. "Oh, my goth."

"What do you see my petite petri dish?" Otis asked. "Any sign of the deceased?"

The mother stepped back and kept her voice low. "I think Orphie should wait in the carriage."

"But mother, I am old enough to see terrible things," the child declared, pounding her feet. "I've already seen the impatiens and the pink mailbox."

"True," calmly replied Otis, "and she was old enough to scare off the missionaries who came to our door last week."

Pyridine nodded, and they snooped to look through the Everydays kitchen window.

Otis shrieked silently, nearly dropping the casket on his feet.

"Yellow dandelions!" gasped Pyridine. She placed her hand over her brow; feeling faint.

Orphie looked at her mother and father in concern, for they always told her, that if someone wearing yellow ever touched you, your skin would burn like a scalding hot iron pressed on flesh.

"I think you better hand over the medicine," insisted Otis.

"But we haven't even met them yet?"

"I know, but I'm afraid I might need it," Otis advised. "Maybe we should turn around, it's not too late." But Orphie was already knocking on their door, and after a few moments, a small upsetting bark rattled them. The parents jumped back, landing again among the impatiens as blood rushed from Otis's other nostril.

The door creaked slightly open, and Orphie curiously tilted closer.

Behind it was a scruffy Chihuahua in a tiny blue tuxedo pulling a sock that had been tied to the doorknob.

The Goodbyes were speechless, perhaps confused by the dog squatting before them and why it dressed so sharply.

"Mister Everyday, I presume?" asked Otis.

"Ruf!"

"I see, someone is on the roof?" he asked. Meanwhile, Orphie bent down and saw the dog collar with the words "Wylie Winks." She stepped inside to explore the house.

Otis looked down at the dog and curled his lip. "My apologies, I did not know you went by your first name. I too prefer Otis over Mister Goodbye, which of course is my father's name, and by seeing how I never really knew him, I would prefer not to be called such a thing. I presume that this may be the same for you?"

"Ruf!"

Orphie interrupted her father, "I don't think that's right."

"Oh yes, my apologies again," responded Otis, "it must be Dr. Rufus Everyday since you are a scientist." Then for a moment, Otis took off his hat and scratched the top of his head in a perplexed manner. He then stepped forward, coming out of a sort of self-induced trance. "Rufus my lad," he acknowledged, "since there is no such name as Ruf unless of course you are made of slate, but then I think you would be called Slater or possibly Siding, but what sort of name is Siding?" The father turned to ponder in thought again. Orphie tugged on his sleeve to try and point out it was merely a dog, but Pyridine hushed the child and whispered, "Let your father do his work. He has much more experience in these kinds of big city relationships."

"Dr. Rufus," Otis carried on, "I understand you must be the man of the house? May I ask to see your spouse?"

"Ruf," the dog barked wagging its tail.

"I see," said Otis disgruntled, "I thought we already established that."

Orphie rose her voice in protest, "What my father means to say is, 'Where is the old bag of bones?'" Which Otis agreed seemed the appropriate thing to say to a dog at the moment. Orphie was a little embarrassed seeing her father in such witlessness, that could be easily corrected; so, Orphie peeked inside and saw her mother examining the deceased woman laid out on the floor, and announced: "Found her."

Otis looked in. "Oh yes," he grinned, highly pleased, and stepped over the incredibly excited Dr. Everyday that nipped at his heels.

Orphie parked the casket beside the rug where the woman's body lay. Mrs. Everyday held in her hands an empty bottle with the inscription Chthonic (pronounced THänik or more simply Tonic, and rhyming with chronic). As Pyridine reached for the container, the dog hopped up on the body to lick the dead woman's face.

"How cute," mused Orphie, "sharing kisses, even at this stage of rigor mortis."

The dog continued to shadow their movement while they worked. "Rufus," batted away Pyridine, "I'm beginning to think you're glad she's dead," she said with anger.

"Yes," said Otis, pointing to Mrs. Everyday's missing ear. "And it seems he has a thing for biting too."

The Chihuahua at this point began jumping wildly on and off the casket.

"All right," scolded Pyridine, trying to shoo away the dog's affection. "Where are your manners?"

After a moment, Pyridine stopped examing the woman. "It appears she was poisoned," Pyridine declared.

"No doubt from overexposure to this ghastly decor," replied Otis.

The brightly colored room was making his head spin. "How can anyone grieve in a room like this? All this color was sure to drive Rufus mad."

Orphie wasn't listening, distracted by the detached ear she found under a sofa. She promptly threw it into the kitchen for the dog to chase, giving Otis and Pyridine enough time to lift Mrs. Everyday off the floor and into the casket, where Rufus could

not reach her. Once the lid was shut, they asked her spouse, the Chihuahua, where her final resting place should be.

"Is there a family plot outside somewhere?" Otis raised his voice.

The dog scampered to the door and pulled the sock to open it. Pyridine and her husband shrugged and followed in the dog's direction; "Maybe he plans to show us."

Orphie hefted the casket over her head and proceeded behind her parents.

The trail ended in the garden, where they saw the Chihuahua circle a tree.

"How very odd," remarked Pyridine. "Do you think he wants her buried under that tree?"

The dog stopped and lifted its leg.

"Wait!" exclaimed Otis. "I think he's pointing."

The dog urinated on the tree and trotted out of sight. The Goodbye family remained speechless. They glanced side-eyed at one another and sat on the casket to discuss the bizarre action. Growing bored, Orphie spoke up: "Let's just bury her at the cemetery with the others."

"Of course! That's a brilliant idea," exclaimed Otis.

Orphie hoisted the casket in the back of the hearse while her parents returned to their carriage seats. It wasn't until Otis picked up the reins he noticed Midnight was no longer attached to them. The horse not only finished her pickle but knocked down the fence and chewed her way through the garden, leaving a path of crushed ornaments.

"Midnight, you must consider a career in landscaping." Pyridine said with a smirk.

"I thought it was odd my nose wasn't bleeding anymore," Otis replied.

Chapter IV. A Cure for All

Meanwhile a day's walk from Slug, Thorne limped to Nicklesworth. A town positioned between a river and rolling hills with slender trees dwindling down to dry patches of farmland.

Thorne watched a large crowd of miners gather around a tall red-roofed wagon with two pipes on its top and the words Chthonic Medicine Show written on its side. On the back porch of the wagon was a sharply dressed man with a pencil-thin mustache and leather fringed coat peddling several bottles at his reach. Peaking out and playing from inside the wagon was a lady pipe organist, presumably who was also its driver. The song 'Savior, Thy Dying Love' played as the peddler spoke.

"Gentlemen," the sharp-dressed man announced, "there is no greater cure for all your ailments than this here bottle of Chthonic. What's it cure you may ask? Everything from a skin rash to an epidemic of disease. Cures diphtheria, diarrhea, dandruff, anything else disadvantageous to your soul!" the man said enchantingly, "Let Chthonic take care of all your worries."

Thorne hobbled closer with the Baron's derby hat on his head and cane in hand.

"Today only, we have free samples for everyone."

Many of the miners were already drunk and pleading for seconds. Thorne used his cane to push through the horde of people with morbid curiosity as the miners clawed toward the last bottles.

Thorne approached the announcer. "You sir," said the man bending down to see Thorne, whose hat covered his pinprick eyes. "I bet you could use a taste. Compliments of your fallen leader, Baron Von Nickle." He bent over and presented the bottle to Thorne with little regard to its receiver. Thorne did not take it, and the peddler quickly recognized the hat that belonged to the Baron and the outlaw to whom he was speaking, and the glare of death staring back at him. "Frank Thorne," he mumbled nervously, staggering back up.

Thorne grabbed ahold of the porch railing and pulled himself up to the stage.

"I know you," said the outlaw, cornering the peddler. "Grissum, wasn't it."

"Cut the music," the man nervously yelled to the organist. The music abruptly stopped.

"Found a new line of work, I see?" Thorne said pointing with the end of the rifle cane to his throat, "No longer in the fur trade business? What'ya getting for all of this. Who's paying you?"

Grissum's face soured, holding up his hands, "If this is about the Baron, I had nothing to do with his death."

"No, no, I suspect you didn't, but you did bring trouble to us. You brought us that little villager named Me'ma that ruined our mine."

"Now you know, we were just trying to help," Grissum said begging for mercy.

"Leave my husband alone," cried the wife pointing a pistol at Thorne, but Thorne was briefly distracted by his darkened reflection in the bottle Grissum still held, that he had not noticed before. He gazed at it intently as the two at arms looked on in confusion. In a flash, Thorne remembered the life he had before his death and the elixir that ended it. A vision of the Baron appeared before Thorne in the bottle speaking to him and erasing his thoughts.

"Manifest," Thorne could hear the Baron say, *"Destroy Grissum, the traitor."*

Thorne turned his eyes back to Grissum and the wife trembling. The crowd was also getting anxious and pushed against the wagon. Thorne grabbed the bottle and broke it over the railing, silencing the audience as he spoke: "This is the man responsible for your loss. He was the one that let the mine cave in. He was the servant that brought the villager and her magic to destroy us."

"No! That's not true. I had nothing to do with that." he said pushing Thorne aside and rushing to hide behind his wife.

Thorne knew the drunken mob could easily be guided and with the sound of the Baron commanding his thoughts, he shouted back: "Take what is yours! Manifest!" Thorne flopped off the porch, leading the crowd into a frenzy. The wagon tipped as Grissum's wife fired a wobbly shot at Thorne. The bullet passed quickly through his shoulder, spraying out his dried dead insides like confetti. The crazed miners pulled their own guns and ripped apart the wagon to get at the last bottles and overtake its hosts. Grissum's wife ran away as her husband was dragged into the street by the onslaught of men. The remaining bottles on board shattered and so too did the people. Bullets went in every direction.

BANG BANG.

CRACK POP.

Shots tore and ripped into Thorne's mummified body.

POP POP POP.

Thorne fired back until the street was silent and filled with the dead. With a hush in the gunfire, Thorne limped to the peddler who was buried under a pile of deceased miners.

"There you are," Thorne said pulling him out with the crook of his cane. "Tell me, where is the man that brought you here?" he demanded.

"No, no. I cannot say."

"You know what I can do to the likes of you," said Thorne reloading his revolver. "You're a miserable creature. A dealer of venom."

"No, we are on the same side." the man pleaded. "I did not start this. I am only taking orders. Just like you. I'm on your side."

"I no longer take orders," said Thorne with gravel in his voice. The peddler saw a chance out of the corner of his eye to flee behind an alley; Thorne could see his eyes shift in its direction and at the moment the peddler sprang, Thorne blasted two shots at the man's knees, dropping him down in an instant.

Thorne could see an unopened bottle of Chthonic gripped in the hands of a dead miner. "Perhaps you should know what it is to be like me," said Thorne. "Let's have you wait here, and drink this," he said tossing him the bottle. "It will help you with your pain. Then, when you bleed out," he said continuing, "it'll be the time for you to wake up. Now take your own medicine."

"No, don't do this to me. Just leave me here."

The peddler looked on in fear as Thorne spoke: "You see, we are not the same. I am death incarnate. I have killed countless vermin like you."

"You won't get away with this," he cried, trying to mend his legs. "No matter how you try, Zenwick will extinguish you."

Thorne choked Grissum and poured the tonic down his throat. "It's important you get a taste of your own medicine." The peddler eventually passed out from shock as the bottle emptied into his mouth.

"Zenwick," Thorne said aloud, "that's a name I haven't heard in a while." Thorne said stirring a memory.

Thorne took hold of the man and dragged him across the dirt with a stagger. He picked up his bullet-ridden hat. He went to each miner's corpse and looted what he could, from new boots to his favorite sugar cubes. Unfortunately, he also found a new whip, but because of his leg and use of the cane, he could not crack it as easily as carrying a firearm. So instead, took it as a memento.

Thorne struggled to carry his plunder, and after checking the pulse of Grissum, decided it was time to cut ties. He saw the sharp broken shards of the bottle and thought of an idea.

When Grissum reawoke in a zombie state, he opened his mouth to let out a scream, but eerily it was buried under moans coming from the dead miners laid scattered and slain across the street. There now corpses crawled into the dark hiding places within the tatters of town.

Chapter V. The Mistaken Heir

The next day, Orphie crawled out of bed and stepped over her tuba, that she enjoyed playing in harmony with her brother's hissing, and made her way downstairs.

Orphie's room was in the attic from where a hatch could be climbed down into a study. This was technically a quarter way up the tree where it had burned inside and halted. A small hole in the tree provided a window for her room to look out over the cemetery. Opposite the study was a curiosity den, with a zigzagging hallway of silhouettes between the rooms that spilled out to the staircase lined with black ribbon. The hallways followed the hollowed branches of the tree as the walls grew smaller to a point. In fact, some places of the tree only Orphie could fit in. She ran down the creaky staircase, passing a coffin corner in the wall, and tiptoed through the master bedroom before skipping through a hall of grisly historical paintings which also acted as a viewing room. This was at the base of the tree. Orphie always stopped in this room to gaze momentarily at the artwork that her mother claimed to have painted and that curiously seemed to move over time. In a few of the paintings she saw: a pirate ship on rough seas, medieval knights jousting, Medusa in her lair, and most puzzling a cue of horseless wagons with their drivers screaming at one another. This was the most frightening of all and caused Orphie to somersault out of the room. From here, she had the option of either opening the door to the right and take steps further down to her mother's laboratory, which in turn was also into the roots of the tree or enter a curtain to the left into a fainting room. Instead, she drew open a third somewhat hidden pocket door at the opposite end of the viewing room and entered their kitchen, where her mother was reading her spell book and counting the last of her ingredients.

"Dreary morning," she said, greeting her mother.

"Dreary afternoon, my progeny," Pyridine corrected with a hug. "It's nearly four pm."

"Is it that late already?" admitted the child, realizing her error.

"Did those horrible garden flowers yesterday make you sleepy?"

"I think so, but I also was up late practicing my tuba."

"Oh, was that all that noise?" her mother asked, "I thought your father was playing a song through his plugged bloody nostrils."

Orphie did not think it odd she slept through the morning and was awake in the evening. Compare the hours of China to the United States; they are at opposite ends of the globe. When we are having breakfast, they are just finishing dinner. When we are asleep, they are only rising. Orphie liked to think she was just following Chinese standards.

"Where did father go?" asked Orphie, picking out a nice thick strand of eye goop.

"He is outside flying his hat," Pyridine laughed and softly pointed to her husband gliding his hat around the yard. The brim of the hat landed briskly across the ground trailing behind Otis, giving it the illusion it had its own feet. Perhaps on closer inspection it had, it was made of caterpillar fur after all.

Orphie opened the front door for her father as he approached with his hat secured in his hands. He tossed the hat in the corner where it greeted Pyridine's magic trocar. Orphie had playfully brought the hat and trocar to life with her mother's potion of Blister Beetle sweat. Pyridine warned that leaving these two alone for too long might produce some ghastly and illogical offspring like a propeller beanie hat. Otis caught his wife's critical squint and snatched the hat away from the trocar.

Otis turned to Orphie and said: "My little vena cava, I thought you'd never wake up?" He bent down and kissed his daughter's forehead. He then turned back to his wife and planted another kiss on her cheek, but Pyridine quickly brushed him away.

"You'll mess up my cosmetics," she said with disappointment.

"Allow me," and she kindly planted a kiss of her own from her palm to Otis's cheek.

"How was your walk, dupa?"

(The family had several different terms of endearment as you will read.)

"I took a trip with my hat down to the Everyday residence," responded Otis, "to see how the widower is coping and collect on the burial costs."

"How is he?" Pyridine said in a despairing tone of voice, "he looked so tired the last I saw him. Did he give you anything for our services?"

"He is splendid," exclaimed Otis in surprise, "he has made some astonishing improvements. The trees are wilted, and the furniture is in shreds."

"Ha," laughed Pyridine, "it seems his spouse was suppressing an inner creative talent after all."

Otis took the bottle of Chthonic left at the Everyday's place and said: "Since he had no money to give me, and he kept barking at the bottle, I figured he wanted me to have that in trade. So we are settled."

"Oh no, Otis." Pyridine said disapprovingly.

He tossed the bottle to his daughter. "Perhaps, you can make it into another instrument." The child's eyes lit up as she blew air over the top of the bottle: *WOOOOO* it resonated in a low pitch.

"That's a perfect fog horn but doesn't pay the rent." Pyridine said regretfully.

"We'll be fine P. We always come through. Things will pick up."

"I fear things are going to get worse before they get better." Pyridine said as her tone dropped. "Look around you. Most of my ingredients are empty. Business has been so bad since the war, we've been having dust soup nearly every night because that's all we can afford."

"But I love your dust soup. I thought you were making it special for me."

"It's terrible father," said Orphie feeding off of her mother's anger. "I miss the old days. We never get to go out anymore. There are many more restaurants in town now."

"Otis, we are several months behind in rent. The Baron will have our heads."

"I don't know where all this is coming from. I feel like I'm being attacked." Otis said in defense.

"Even if we had the money to bury Mrs. Everyday we couldn't," said Pyridine.

Otis looked down at his wife's neckline. "I don't see any specks of hair or skin flakes. What happened?"

"This morning I was working on Mrs. Everyday and found that she didn't die of alcohol poisoning. Even though she consumed large amounts of Chthonic before death. Rather it appears she was strangled. I was going to tell you that, but you already left. That's when I came back and saw Mrs. Everyday had completely vanished!"

"Vanished? In this world, dead things don't just get up and walk out." Otis said, sniffing the air.

"You don't suspect our son Kepla got ahold of her?" she replied. "There's really no way of knowing where she might be. Kepla's such a recluse. At least he eventually buries his toys in the cemetery."

Otis shrugged.

"Outside of that conundrum, we received a package at our front door."

"Did we lose another mail carrier in the process?"

"No, as that might pay the bills."

(Orphie used to build booby traps around the yard and not tell anyone until someone fell into them. It was disastrous for those visiting, but an excellent way for the Goodbyes to meet their neighbors).

"Oh no, they never come around anymore. One of our crow friends must have dropped it off."

"May I see?" asked Orphie like a child to candy.

"I don't see why not," said Pyridine. "Follow me, I've taken it to the lab."

The three descended a spiraling staircase and entered the lab. The tree home's massive root system had overtaken one wall of the basement and interwoven itself into a perfect built-in shelf which Pyridine found most convenient for bottles, jars, and her various laboratory implements. A table with surgical tools was positioned on the far side of the roots next to a sheet-covered gurney bearing a mysterious small mound.

Pyridine walked closer and lowered the sheet. Otis and Orphie leaned closer in excitement. "Perhaps it's someone's pet?" asked Otis.

"No," Pyridine groaned. "At least not a whole one." She revealed three oily strands of braided hair.

"Rattails."

The child peered at it. "A rat with three tails?! I want one!"

"Nope, seems to be human," remarked Otis thoughtfully, taking out an eyeglass to examine it. The spectacles were held inside a pocket within a pocket, sewn by hand into a third smaller pocket. "I'll take notes."

Otis walked over to the exposed roots of the ancient tree in the basement of the house. He placed his hat on a sturdy root while he broke off a dry paper-like root and took the feather from his hat and dipped it into his greasy hair like a quill to ink.

The roots of the tree must have spanned the entire countryside, and at which each twig of root could be unraveled and written on like a scroll.

Orphie inspected the rattails under her mother's microscope. "I see something! Mother, have a look!"

Under the lens, Pyridine could see tiny bugs on an ever-so-small ritzy bug bar drinking and raising a toast with a little champagne bottle.

"Oh, my goth," she exclaimed and increased the magnification. "They're drinking the expensive stuff."

"What year?" Otis asked, bending over the scope.

Pyridine quickly plucked a hair from Otis's head. "Youch!" he cried. "Whatcha' do that for?"

"For science," she responded. "Now take a look at one of your father's hairs under the scope." The three examined again.

"Prosecco," screamed Otis in horror.

"No, even worse," said Pyridine. "Seltzer. I suspect on the rattails we are dealing with bourgeois lice. Very, very uncommon around here."

"There is only one person I know who would carry such a louse..."

"Baron Von Nickle?"

"Precisely," declared P. "And he wouldn't go around town without his locks."

"What's he baring?" asked Orphie innocently.

"Not much I'm certain," said the mother. "He is likely deceased."

"Then there goes our troubles! I guess we don't have to pay rent," Otis wisely commented, hopping in joy.

"Or rent just went up," Pyridine remarked holding him down. "Depending of course on the new owner." She paused and reflected, "I wonder if someone wants these relic rattails made into a ring or necklace. That may bring us a pretty penny?"

Otis took the strands in his hand and placed them over his head. "What do you think? Do they do make handsome extensions?" as Orphie chuckled with him.

"Hmpfh. We should see if someone wants to claim the hair," Pyridine replied, rubbing her palms wishfully, "I'm certain the Baron has many wealthy friends in town we can charge for giving him the very best Victorian memento."

Otis rose a finger and announced: "I'll head into Nicklesworth and see if I can dredge something up," He set his notes aside and placed the feather back onto his hat to wear. Pyridine proceeded to take the rattails and knotted them around her husband's right-handed pinkie finger, into a reminder's knot, knowing his bouts of forgetfulness could strike at any time. "Remember my bat, find a buyer that pairs well with the bourgeois lice, and that may save us for the time being."

Chapter VI. Otis in Nicklesworth

Otis rode his carriage as far as the cemetery of Nicklesworth. He could see ahead in the town the streets were littered with broken furniture, glass from windows, and pieces of a burned out building. It appeared that a terrible riot had taken place earlier.

Otis mindfully parked alongside an abandoned cart and took his funeral bag with him in case anyone needed an immediate undertaking. He strolled into the town as people hid and others like the miners wandered around to loot. Otis could see the steamboat had sunk. A few miners stumbled by the dock. Otis could tell they were wildly intoxicated, probably from the bottles that were strewn about. Some were in the calico underclothes, and missing boots or hats, while others only had their hats to cover themselves.

Oblivious to their living-death, Otis happily carried on and greeted them. "Dreary day," he said tipping his hat. "Looks like rain is on its way!"

Otis approached the riverboat's captain who sat hunched over asleep clutching an empty bottle. Otis squatted in front of the man and lifted the drunkards' chin.

"Hello Captain Miles, I'm sure you are flooded with a deluge of emotion," said Otis encouragingly, "but don't look so adrift. Drowning in a bottle will never do." Otis took the bottle from him. "Stick a little boat inside here, and you'll have your ship back." Otis threw the bottle into the water to prove his point. "See it floats."

The captain slouched back intoxicated.

"Here, have a cigar on me," said Otis taking a pickle from his pocket and placing it into the Captain's mouth.

Continuing on his way, Otis strangely kept seeing the same empty bottle caressed in the grasp of others strewn over the town. "Chthonic," Otis read the label of the bottle aloud to himself. He turned the bottle in his hand to read the back as the print became smaller with each word: "Cure all for disorders of the mind and body; specifically sluggish liver, rheumatism, lumbago, gouty pains, bronchitis, sore throat, sciatica, neuralgia, nausea, dizziness, vomiting, cholera, overwhelming thirst, cramps, syphilis, measles, mumps, diphtheria, rubella, scarlet fever, a girl named Scarlet, rash, smallpox, typhus, tuberculosis...," and this explanation went on and on as he questioned if something so grand could really cure anything. "That's a new one," he said taking a whiff and dropping it, "smells like the backside of a bison."

Otis used his nose to proceed down an alley that was currently more of a makeshift coma ward, miners huddled half- unconscious. He checked them as he went but none seemed to have expired, except for one by chance that was completely missing - the sheriff, and this Otis found as the shiny star he wore was the only thing left from him sticking up in the dirt.

Otis looked down at his reminder's knot which jolted his memory. He decided to visit the blacksmith, a man who knew everyone in town. He quickly saw the shop had not been immune to the looters. The doors had been ripped open and most inside had been cleared out - including the blacksmith and his wagons.

Unknowingly above him, Frank Thorne stared down at him from the hayloft. Thorne was now wearing the very best stolen clothes in town and the Baron's derby hat. Only the head of Mr. Grissum remained, which he dropped down in front of Otis.

THUD!

Otis mistakenly plodded into the head tripping over it: "Hey watch where you're going," the head of Grissum rolled to say, "can't you see I'm standing here." Otis raised a brow. "Standing, sitting, something," he said in shock, before gazing up to meet the eye of Thorne. Thorne's face was bulging with open scars and a deep dead purple vein. His sunken and blackened eyes framed the specter of glowing fire inside.

"Excuse me," the outlaw spoke matter-of-factly. "I must have dropped that."

But Otis took no offense. "You know, I had a cousin Dribble that was always losing his head. It would knock off on door frames, tree branches, you name it. We blamed his body for being the clumsily one."

"The kicker was," Otis continued, "his head traveled the world, while his body was really holding him back, we said Dribble you should have quit while you were a-head."

"Enough!" Thorne shouted swatting hay down at Otis with his cane.

Otis blew the hay off his hat and wiped his shoulders. "But don't you want your ball back?"

"I got what I need out of him," Thorne said popping a sugar cube in his mouth.

"While I have you," Otis continued, "might I ask, are either one of you, the head of things around here? I have a precious memento I'm looking to pawn."

"You don't say." Thorne gruffed. The head perched silently.

"I do," he said presenting it into view. "It's the Baron's rattails."

"How did you find those?"

"No lookie, no peekie," Otis replied without concern. "I only show to interested buyers."

Thorne suspected the buffoon of a bean pole standing below him could interfere with his plans, and instead of addressing Otis with a threat, he lifted his arms into the air and uttered but one command. "Manifest." The word that the Baron repeated in his head and came much more evident to him with the derby hat on.

Within an instant, the miners who appeared asleep in the street were awakened. Their beaten and injured bodies hobbled and hopped towards Otis, including the head that was now rolling towards with chomping teeth!

Otis's returning eyes were met by a menacing swarm that approached. "Evening," he said to the crowd while trying to shake the head from biting him, but instead of a response, they proceeded to place their hands over Otis as if to strangle him. Their pale blue hands showed the way to their dead faces.

Thorne suspected Otis might be reaching into his vest for a gun, but pulled out something green that reeked of vinegar.

"Anyone care for a pickle?" he said kindly, presenting them to the mob before realizing they were not going to quit. The loft above slammed shut, throwing more hay over Otis.

"If you don't mind, this little hoedown is a little dry for my taste," he said backing up into the barn. The crowd pushed through and forced Otis to climb up the loft to where Thorne had appeared and now exited.

"Zombies? No wonder our business has been hurting."

The people continued up the ladder chasing Otis. Most of the crowd had made their way into the barn, and Otis fended off those he could from the ladder and was able to launch the head which was still biting his pant leg at the horde. "Firing cannons!" he yelled, kicking the head at the zombies. It did little good as they continued upward and gave Otis no other option but to jump out of the window.

He placed his magic stovetop hat over his head and glided down safely like a short distance parachute. He locked the barn doors and saw across the street the saloon's lights. He ran to its safety and inside saw the room filled with battered chairs and tables lying about over the bar and floor with shards of the Chthonic bottles between them.

"This is an improvement from that crowd," Otis said timidly. With no danger in sight, he pushed the saloon's piano in front of the doors and stopped to regain his breath.

"Howdy Mr. Goodbye," yelled out someone in the room, causing Otis to jump.

Otis hunted for the voice and panned above him to see a familiar saloon girl hanging from the ceiling chandelier. "Where have ya been stranger?" she shouted again.

"Is that you Miss Blu?" Otis said, recognizing the dancer.

"Does a cow 'udder'?"

Miss Emma Blu dressed in a blue corset with a blue lily on her head. It was uncertain if the flower grew from her skull naturally or was just pinned to it. Nevertheless, she did not know how to fly, so it was unusual to see her in this precarious position.

"How did you get up there?" Otis asked. "Is that a new part of your act?"

"No, silly," replied Emma, "I must have blacked out, and someone threw me up here. Now, are you going to help me down or what?"

Otis surveyed his surroundings for a stool or something sturdy to stand on but could only produce two empty Chthonic crates. He stacked the boxes together and climbed atop to assist the lady down into his hands. Miss Blu nervously swung from his shoulders to her feet.

"Thank you kindly," said the dancer, kissing the ground, "You don't know how grateful I am to be touching the earth again. I was beginning to feel a little high-minded if you understand me."

"I can see that," Otis said with a heavy breath. "The whole town has gone mad. Where's the rest of your gang, did the stiffs get them?"

In reply, Miss Blu whistled and hollered. "Professor Lint, the coast is clear."

Otis turned to see the pianist warily emerge from within the piano top. "I hope for our sake, it is."

"We have an audience," said Miss Blu to her piano player. Lint wore a lab coat covering a tightly fitted vest, round eyeglasses, a flat cap and a kilt in matching blue.

"Professor is he?" asked Otis, thinking of his potential for wealth.

"Oh no, he just likes to be called that. He's a professor of the saloon." The dancer said, posed with her arms behind her back and instructed to her accomplice: "Let's start with a D and go up," referring to the notes she was about to climb vocally.

"Arpeggio," the professor dragged a three-legged chair to sit on. He then took out a cedar guitar from inside the piano top as Otis watched leaning against the bar. With this, Miss Blu unveiled a massive fan she was hiding behind her back and began tapping her feet wildly in a flamenco style, jumping to and fro between the broken furniture. Faint drumming indicated it was coming from under the bar as Otis sat mesmerized watching Miss Blu sing the following verse:

A miner's greatest fear is a cave in.
Yes sir, I claim it to be true.
The day they lost it all,
The Baron took a fall
And the miners came back pannin' for a coup.
Twas at night they were pickin' for a fight.
Yes sir, I claim it to be true.
They raided our saloon,
Started lickin' our spittoon,
They were acting like a big ol' bag of foo's.

The professor took over and proceeded to sing in a solo:

At night they ran out of tonic.
Yes sir, I claim it to be true.
They consumed it like fleas,
Left their worry to oilies...

It was then both the professor and Miss Blu pressed their backs together and sang while slinking down to their bottoms:

Yes sir, they were comatose before curfew.

They were startled by a faint uproarious cheer coming from under the bar. The three followed her to the source, stepping over the litter. The clapping continued inside an empty Chthonic barrel. Otis took a small hammer from one of his pockets - the one he used for nailing coffins and pried open the barrel's lid. Inside, a bartender who they called Hibiscus doubled over with his feet right in front of his bald head. He had just enough space to make a tiny sound with his hands. Otis pulled him out, finding him quite drunk from what remained in the barrel.

"Thank you." said the bartender with a hiccup. "I'm sorry no more tonics left, fresh out."

Otis thumbed to the street. "Seems like it is a real knockout," Otis answered, flaunting the knotted rattails with a wave of his little finger.

Hibiscus gasped aloud and pressed a hand to his bald head. "You found my hair!" The bartender reached for Otis's pinky nearly pulling it out of the socket. Thankfully, the professor yanked the bartender back, loosened his grip and scolded: "Control yourself, your hair was lost ages ago. Besides it was never braided."

"Whose hair is it then?" the bartender sulked. Otis laughed and said: "You'll have to see this Hiccupus," mistakenly naming him and taking out the eyeglass from one of his many pockets to show the hair under magnification.

"Great Mountain!" said Miss Blu. "What are those?"

"Bourgeoisie lice," Otis responded.

"I never heard of such a thing," declared Professor Lint, in high alarm.

"That's because they are rare," Otis said, staring at the jovial lice which were linked in a chorus line doing a hurdy-gurdy. "And the only thing left of the Baron."

"No happiness comes from keeping his things," returned Miss Blu in a surly tone.

"I do not intend to keep them," Otis replied, "I need to sell the mementos to a Baron's heir."

"Hair!" Hibiscus yelled. "Where? I saw it first." He tried to grab them again, thinking he meant hair versus heir, turning Otis towards the drunk with his eyeglass. "I knew it. I knew it!" The bartender shouted, "That was never his hair. It's mine I tell ya. Give it back," the bartender cried.

"Control yourself!" Miss Blu said slapping his hands. "His heir, his benefactor. Not your hair. Go sober up."

"Must you be so recessive?" The bartender said staggering to the floor to sit. "Hiccup." Several more words mumbled from the man's mouth as he put his leg over a keg and continued to converse sweetly to a barrel spout.

Otis wiped the eyeglass, and shook his head at the pathetic yet joyful state of the man before turning to start again: "I guess my question is, did the Baron have any heirs?" said he, placing the eyeglass back into his pocket.

Suddenly Hibiscus blared out: "Miss Blu's beau!"

"No," she recoiled.

"Which one?" mumbled the Professor.

"No one is to speak HIS name." Miss Blu folded her arms.

"Ah that one," the Professor said, being careful not to speak his name. "They were engaged," he said looking at Miss Blu to make sure he could tell her story. Seeing no violent reaction from her, he continued, "But that fool became engrossed in that tonic. You saw what it does. He went mad and left town without her."

"A real deal breaker," the bartender suggested moving in to kiss the spout he caressingly sat beside.

He nodded in acknowledgment and said in a more cheery voice:

"How did the Baron know him?"

"He was his son." Emma snorted with anger.

"Wow, the man you fell in love with was the Baron's father. I don't want to judge, but that's awfully old for you, isn't it." Otis replied.

"No, you goof. It's the other way around. He had a falling out with his father. He never told me why. So he took his mother's maiden name instead." She slammed her fan on the bar. "I don't want to hear any more about him. I want him outta my life forever."

Otis thought in reflection and asked ignorantly. "I suppose you don't know where he is?"

"Really, must you be so dim," exclaimed Miss Blu. "Some infernal place I hope!"

"Oh?" said Otis with interest. "Sounds delightful."

Everyone looked at Otis peculiarly, thinking he might also be deranged. But while Emma wept, Otis volunteered to help Hibiscus sober up, forcing him to eat jars of pickled food from haunches and hominy to eggs, among other things from Purple Leaf Selects. A meal that was so detested it could sober up anyone.

The three yawned, and Otis feeling drowsy, sat down, tipping the last intact chair back against the wall. "You don't suppose we can take a nap?" said Otis. Weary and in desperate need of rest. Suddenly they were rattled upright by a racket against the walls.

POUND, POUND, POUND.

The zombie crowd had escaped the barn and were punching through the saloon walls. One of the zombies broke through and momentarily took hold of Miss Blu.

"Let her go, you stiff!" cried the Professor.

The professor vaulted over the trash and smacked the guitar over the zombie's head, obliterating the instrument into pieces. It really was his best solo as Miss Blu was released and the four raced out the back door.

Chapter VII. The Plan

Otis boarded Emma, Lint, and Hibiscus in the carriage and gave Midnight a handful of pickles to quicken her pace home. They arrived the next evening to find Pyridine drinking Toadstool tea on the porch steps.

"What took so long Dupa, and who are these visitors?" asked Pyridine.

Otis shivered as he stood over his wife on the steps. "This is Emma Blu, Professor Lint, and Hibiscus. They run the saloon in town, or what is left of it."

"Oh yes, I do know you. Please have a seat. I'm afraid I don't have a cup of tea for each of you. I only just found a mushroom today near the outhouse to make the tea. Things have been desperate around here recently. Are you okay if it's watered down?" Pyridine said, pouring them each a cup as they sat on the stairs.

"Quite alright," they agreed.

She then placed a cup into Otis's shaky hands and saw the rattails were missing.

"Where is the hair?" said Pyridine looking at him sternly. "Did you not make the sale? Oh no, Otis, of all things."

Otis scratched his head and looked around at the group. Hibiscus was wearing the rattails over his forehead and sadly returned it to Pyridine.

"So do you want the good news or the bad news?"

"We could use some good news," answered his wife.

"I smell a torrential rainstorm is heading our way," declared Otis.

"Oh, yes, that is positive," she replied with a sigh. "We haven't had a good downpour in years. And then what else is the bad news?" Her brow raised in concern.

Otis paused and rose his cup of watered-down toadstool tea to his nose and sniffed it to try and wash out the rainy scent.

"The mine caved in, and the people of Nicklesworth went nuts. And dead people were walking everywhere. Not one to bury," he said looking glum.

"A ghost town and no one to bury? Otis, you're not making sense."

"He's telling the truth. Not ghosts, zombies!" piped up Emma.

"With terrible drinking problems." seconded the professor.

Pyridine nearly spilled her tea: "This is highly abnormal for this world. How are we going to afford to replenish our potions and supplies? I expected you to help me." she said crossly. "How can we make a living without anyone staying dead enough to bury!"

"I don't know my bat. I don't know. It worries me also," agreed Otis trying to calm her. He then noticed the fragrant flower in Emma's hair and wisely changed the subject.

"How was Mrs. Everydays wake?" he enquired. "Did anyone notice Mrs. Everyday was not present?"

"No, it was a closed casket, and Orphie was bothering the mourners again. It's our neighbors for goth's sake," she replied, sitting back down, "I don't know how many times we have to tell her playtime is not during our services." When the family hosted a wake, Orphie could be grossly playful. They often had to remind the child to "pay your respects." But since she was a spritely child, her best was about as good as smiling at a mourner and tugging on their jacket to whisper, "you smell like mothballs." Even still it was better than her more mischievous acts, which included blowing out candles, crawling up behind the seated guests and tickling the back of their necks, or hiding under the casket and knocking.

"Good gracious!" cried Otis, shrinking back into the bench. "What did she do this time?"

"She started playing Chopin's funeral march on her tuba during the wake, stirring the guests into a panic."

"Oh," said Otis relieved, "I thought you were going to say she was playing hide and shriek with her brother."

Pyridine nodded. She looked at her husband with big eyes and said: "You know the last heavy rain was many moons ago."

"That's right," gasped Otis, in wonder; "the last rain brought many bugs, rodents, and pests inside our house to stay warm. It was a menagerie of creatures nesting."

"We were ill-equipped, to say the least."

Otis shook his head. "Would hate to go through that again."

"We get them all the time at the saloon, a real nuisance," said Emma.

"We had to set traps to keep them from taking over," replied Professor Lint.

"No, on the contrary, we enjoy their company. My concern is that we will not have a crumb in the house for any of them to eat."

The saloon workers looked strangely at the Goodbyes.

It was then, Otis sat the cup aside and turned to Pyridine remembering something Miss Blu had said. The Baron's son and heir of the three strands of hair supposedly lived in 'an infernal place,' or at least he took it literally to be so. And not only was the Lake of Fire an infernal place, but he also was reminded of their engagement and remembered it was at the Lake of Fire he proposed to Pyridine. Otis brushed his goatee softly thinking how nice it would be to rekindle that flame. "I have an idea," he said aloud.

"Is it to close up shop and hide our heads in shame?" said Pyridine.

"No, no," said Otis, "there is still time for that." He stood and placed his fists on his hips. "The seed of a great plan has just been dropped into my brain. Allow the worms and fluids to foster its growth, and I'll share my idea in the morning." He then promptly threw up the tea which was too strong for his  stomach. He hunched over and dropped to the porch hugging it. Pyridine shrugged, leaving Otis heaving and shuddering spread-eagle on the porch. "Come along," she said, directing their guests to step over Otis's sudden nausea. "Let's find a place for you to sleep."

"Is he okay?" said Miss Blu.

"Yes, he's fine. He always does this when he gets an idea. It's such a shock to his body, he vomits."

Chapter VIII. The Old Cemetery

It was now early morning, and Pyridine checked on Emma, Lint, and Hibiscus, whom found it easier to sleep in the funeral parlor than in the guest rooms. She called upstairs to Orphie who was playing her tuba. "Come down my little bat; your father has something to share."

"What are you conjuring?" asked Pyridine. "Can't I get a hint. We won't have to sell Orphie to the circus or borrow from the general store, will we?"

Otis smiled and suggested, "Be patient."

Orphie slid down the banister with enthusiasm, meeting her parents at their feet. "Yes, daddy?"

Otis knew if he said the plan simply involved delivering the rattails they might not go for it. So instead proposed: "It is coming upon the time of the blood moon and that of, course, is our anniversary. With your agreement, I'd like to do something special this year."

"Are you joking? We can't afford anything right now," argued Pyridine. "Keep dreaming."

"That's what I'm getting at," said Otis. And then he added, with some anxiety: "I propose a business trip!"

"Oh father, not one of those." Orphie groveled. "They are never fun, they always end up with you searching for the best outhouse."

"No, no," he corrected, "it would be different, to gather supplies the old fashioned way. So we don't have to purchase them. We can write off the whole trip!" Otis panned around the room and rushed to pick up an empty bottle. "We could go to the Pit of Despair to catch Blister Beetles."

"They would make good snacks, and we can always use their sweat for our elixirs." He then raced to another corner of the room and took in his hands what appeared to be a fan made out long bug wings. "Then we could pluck a wing of the elusive Giant Borrelia for your potions and its leftovers would make a delicious entree."

Orphie clapped her hands delightedly as her mouth began to water. Pyridine stood with her arms crossed.

Otis reached out and shook another bottle near him. Specks of dust and a dead fly fell into his palm. He twirled them together in his hand. "With a hint of spoiled sulfur for seasoning." He dashed to the cabinet and pinched a small bit of mold, before sitting crisscross on the floor. "And for dessert," he presented the mold and popped it into his mouth. "Moldy Melon slugs from Hemlock Canyon, covered in a Bearded Bree sauce!"

"No, we mustn't, that is way too decadent." Pyridine frowned.

"How about pitohui on the pink pitohui's in Strychnine City?" begged Otis.

"I don't know," Pyridine unfolded her arms, "you made that up? Anyways, we have so much to do here. It would take a lifetime to gather all of our supplies." She gazed around the room and could see many of her potions were in a sad state.

"We must," Otis argued.

"We mustn't," insisted his wife.

"Must!" piped Orphie.

"It is rather musty in here." Otis said sniffing the air before turning back to the attention of his beloved, sweetly adding, "You could collect whatever else you need as we travel. What is a proper apothecary without henbane and eye of Cyclops?"

Pyridine contemplated the empty containers lining her pantry. "I am nearly out of everything." She shook her head disapprovingly. "It's terribly long and who will look after the house while we are gone?"

"The way I see it, Emma, Lint, and Hibiscus need time to reflect so they can house sit," Otis said turning to the parlor. "Besides, I know a shortcut," remarked Otis, "And if we need to save money, we can stay with your family along the way."

"Your shortcuts take twice as long."

"Can we?" asked Orphie shaking her mother's arms.

Pyridine paused and made a final decision. "Fine. I will pack the Baron's rattails and a few other unidentified criminal bodies, John and Jane Doe's, in case we come upon a free burial spot. We cannot continue to conduct funerals without pay!"

"Good idea P." Otis said in victory, "That would save us time and is a direct trip. Reminds me of the saying, a stitch in time saves nine. Let's take nine, and boy they are all stitched up."

"Makes perfect sense. Let's notify our families." She returned in conflicted joy. Pyridine looked down at her fingers. She wore several black celluloid rings with faces of their SAD relatives, an acronym for Still Avoiding Death - witches, warlocks and other undead members of the family. These were similar to picture mourning rings but were quite magical, and she kept all her favorite relatives in them which she was in touch with just like a telephone (notably before its time).

"Yeast," she summoned, looking down at the ring that contained her mother-in-law.

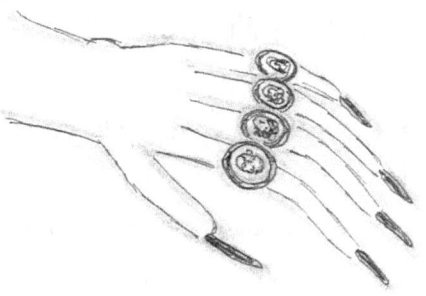

"One second!" The head in one of the ring's answered back. "I've got a cat crisis," and for a moment disappeared.

Yeast could be still heard talking to her countless cats that were meowing loudly in the background. "Lucifer get down from there! I can't believe I need to clean the ash litter again. I just did!" Yeast tended a farm of cats of various sizes and types and was both their caretaker and servant. She was short in stature and wore dresses covered in cat hair, and wore a wig made of the same. It was unclear if she meant to wear the wig or if it simply collected on her scalp. Her eyes were red and weepy from allergies and the hair collected on her eyelashes, making them extra long. She was extra spritely and sat on a ladder to lift herself up from the cats to talk:

"Hello Pyridine!"

"Your son, Otis, has the wise idea to visit." Pyridine returned.

"Splendid!" Yeast exclaimed.

"Might we stay with you on the third night of the blood moon?" asked Pyridine peering down at her.

Yeast momentarily paused and could be heard asking her cats in secret if it would be acceptable to which she came back to the ring and said: "Certainly, the cats said you can sleep in their room."

"Oh," Pyridine said with false excitement, "how dreadful." Pyridine continued ringing up all her favorite relatives notifying them about their trip as Otis and Orphie began packing.

After shoveling down a quick breakfast of dust soup, the family stood beside the carriage. "Did you leave some crickets out for Kepla?" Pyridine asked the child.

"Yes, mother." Orphie placed a few dried crickets and dead wasps on a plate atop the kitchen table. Thinking if Kepla wouldn't eat it perhaps the guests, might for their breakfast.

"Thank you, my little bat. Now could you give your father a hand with the casket?"

Orphie carried the coffin carrying the deceased together over her head, while Pyridine secured the occupants - including the rattails for stress. Otis fed Midnight another pickle.

"What are the people like where we are going?" Orphie asked, taking her place beside her father, where she had the best view.

Otis looked back in surprise. "They are a little upside down, but they are no different from us. They want the same things."

"What's that, father?"

"A slow death, a full restraint and the pursuit of tireless misery."

Pyridine spoke up through the window, "I hope you don't mind, but I thought I'd pack a few urns also in case we come across their Wishful End."

"That's a good idea P; you never know when we'll find the right place for them. Besides, the town of Wishful End is not that far from our destination."

Otis led the carriage to their backyard cemetery where several crows and Pyridine's pet trocar and Otis's hat flew low behind following their path.

The hearse stopped at a green mound, where unbeknownst to Orphie, Walter Nothom was laid to rest. Nothom was Orphie's favorite folk hero, the legendary cattle poacher who had a monopoly on every ranch, robbing their ranges, not with a team of thieves, but solely with his forty-foot height. The opposing ranchers that resisted could do very little as he picked the cows up like candy. But one day, he fell of old age and was buried with an unmarked grave at the very spot the carriage pulled up to in the shadow of the Great Mountain. Amid the mound, whereabouts his foramen magnum, or the hole at the base of his skull, was piled a flat rock. Orphie was told the Great Mountain was actually the family burial plot of the entire Nothom clan, with Walter being the most recent and last to roam the land. They had been buried with bent knees. The layers of dirt blanketed the giants with their ascending bent knees forming its peaks.

Orphie was puzzled to stop, "Are we gathering more crickets?"

"No, no," said her father with a laugh, "this is our short cut." Otis jumped off the carriage as Orphie peered over the carriage roof watching her father approach the grave.

"What are you doing?" She called down.

"Patience," said Pyridine, through the carriage window, "let your father do his work."

Otis took from his pocket a set of gold keys, one of which read 'Home' and the second 'Nothom.' He carefully lurched over and placed the 'Nothom' key into the letter "t" of the "Nothom" name on the marker and turned it clockwise. He heard a painful groan that meant it unlocked, however also noticed the grave marker had a hole under it as if something burrowed its way in.

"Mysterious," said Otis aloud. "Must have rabbits digging in the cemetery again." The hole, however, was larger than any rabbit's, and he could see that a person could squeeze through the makeshift opening. Otis, with the help of Midnight tied the flat grave marker to the back of the hearse and threw a pickle a few steps ahead of the horse. Midnight reaching for the vegetable pulled the carriage. It was slow at first, and Otis looked concern, but after a minute he saw the horse and carriage move again as Orphie got behind the carriage and was pushing it ahead.

"Your strength never ceases to amaze me," he said with a chuckle.

The gravestone slid open from the grave, revealing underneath a passageway large enough for the hearse to pass through.

"Father, where does this tunnel go?"

"To Nothom of course," chimed the father. He climbed back into the driver's seat. "Pyridine, would you be kind enough to light the carriage lanterns?"

Pyridine took out four matches from her dress pocket. She proceeded to light each candle fixture outside the hearse windows. Orphie returned to the roof where she laid out above her father, while Otis sniffed the air and with another quick throw of a pickle and a raspberry, lifted the reins of Midnight and led the hearse into the void.

Chapter IX. Entering Nothom

The candles flickered, and the Goodbye family drove through a long passage bracketed at first with giant bone then leading into carefully stitched needlepoint. A variety of strange tiny creatures were pinned to the yarn in patterns of flowers, gravestones, and grieving women. The walls were canvased in Vulcanite Bee-roaches, from the floor to the ceiling; while the ceiling contained Jet Earring-wigs, and the floor Bog Oak Button-flies. Ahead they passed through dense leaflets hanging from the bony rafters that tickled but did not stick to the passengers. The leaflets became more constant, and the brushing wobbled the carriage.

After a short distance, Otis said he felt queasy and had to stop the carriage momentarily, trying to overcome his sickness: "Let's take a breather," he belched, "I think this is a decent place to stop." Otis had another idea.

"But we just started?" Orphie protested.

"No better time to reflect on where we've been," said her mother.

"But we haven't gone anywhere!" asserted the child. "That is a contradiction."

"Quite the diction indeed," Otis murmured through the handkerchief he held over his mouth.

Pyridine poked through the window. "My dole," she said affectionately to her daughter, "your father means to vomit."

"Can I watch?" Orphie said.

Otis had a method of calming his stomach by slicking his mustache with a comb made of pterodactyl teeth. He brushed his mustache three times, then breathed in and out six times, before repeating the process entirely. But he was not so much sick as he was acting - for his ultimate plan was to find the perfect jeweled gift to give to Pyridine to rekindle the flame at the Lake of Fire.

"Let's take a look at the osteology," Pyridine suggested to Orphie as the daughter climbed down and helped her mother out of the back of the stuffed hearse. The two held hands and examined the exquisite embroidery. Pyridine traced her fingernails over the fragment of insects stuck for eternity. "Fascinating," she mumbled. Here and there, she took samples of bugs for her ingredients, while Otis made sure he was far ahead of her to find the right present before she saw it.

"Perhaps," wondered Orphie, "this is what Nothom had a hard time digesting." Pyridine was not so certain and chipped away a piece of a fossilized Onyx Neck-lice into a medicine bottle. Orphie meanwhile skipped away looking for other oddities, hoping to find something creepier.

It was then, a little distance from the carriage Orphie heard a squeaky voice come from a canvas above. She raced over and saw what she thought was a simple bat. "Mother," exclaimed Orphie, promptly calling her over. But there further into the tunnel she found a webbed valance and stuck in the middle, a tiny winged creature covered in oil. Its little voice chirped like a squirrel as it thrashed around in the trap.

Without waiting, Otis placed something into his pocket and ran to the child, meeting her with awe at the drooping valance. It was dimly lit, so Otis coerced Midnight closer with a pickle. The passage blazed in a light reflecting off a pinned pattern of Die-Mound Ants, being able to see the creature clearly.

"Don't look directly at the Die-Mound Ants," Pyridine warned, they have a hypnotic effect."

Heeding Pyridine's advice, Otis and Orphie focused on the unusual creature. It was not pinned but rather entangled in the canvas yarn. It had the head of a small apple and the body of a crab apple branch with red leaves for wings. Its tiny knot hands held a miniature scythe (that being a twig with a long thorn on its end) and on its feet were seeds for boots. As mentioned its body was covered in oil blackening out its normally bright red appearance.

"What is it?" asked the father, searching for his eyeglass with a smile. "Did you find a Chromis humbug perchance?" He lifted the glasses to his eye. Otis knew the Chromis humbug was his wife's favorite species and worn proudly before it was lost in the house fire.

"I wish," said Pyridine, looking at Otis who was curiously smiling.

"I don't think it's an insect," commented the child. "More doll-like than anything."

"Do you think he intends to harvest wheat?"

Pyridine stepped forward and pointed her sharp fingernail through the yarn. "Now that is strange," she said seeing it closer, "a Giant Borrelia."

"Bored all of us," asked Orphie.

"No, Giant Borrelia," corrected the father, trying to sound intelligent, "the tsetse fly of Nothom. They linger to remind its residents of their immortality."

"Oh yea," returned the child. "We were going to pluck its wing for the party?"

"But why is it drenched in oil?" Pyridine stated, removing one of its leafy wings with a quick pinch and twist, and thereby releasing the creature out of the yarn. "It is quite far from its sour habitat." She said placing the wing in a specimen jar.

The Borrelia, with a small bit of yarn still attached to its shoulders, appearing like a scarf, flew down and unleashed the tiny scythe at the family. "Musba, Musba!" It said shrieking, swinging the weapon.

"What a crab," said Orphie, backing away.

"No, I think that's just his way of welcoming us." Otis attempted to return the formality at the creature but accidentally knocked it to the ground. "Musba, Musba," he replied excitedly.

"Do you suppose he speaks in tongues?" said Orphie.

"Ah, the universal language of love," replied the mother with a laugh, "Can't say I know that word though, perhaps he is cursing us. I did take one of his wings, after all. But a plucked wing for freedom is a fair trade, isn't it?"

The Borrelia felt dizzy and in defeat turned its shaken head and fluttered sideways out of sight and up towards the earth's surface.

"Bravo, bravo," they said clapping. "A real performer, a true illusionist!"

It was then, Orphie could feel something crawl onto her hair. The child placed her hand over it and brought it down before her eyes. The crafter. The exhibitor. The artist of all the glorious needlepoint around them was cupped in Orphie's hands.

"A Needlework Tarantula!" Pyridine quickly called out. "What a rare specimen!"

"Boy, that is a real treat," Otis smiled.

"Hello, my fangy friend." The child lowered the spider away from her eyes, in case it accidentally shed its back hair. In reply, the spider crawled up her arm and planted itself again into her scalp.

"It seems to like your hair," said Pyridine. "It is rather thin and wispy."

"Okay," she replied firmly, "I guess if it is meant to stay a while, I should name it."

"How about Orphie?" suggested Otis.

"But that's my name," reminded his daughter.

"Oh, is that why that name makes me smile?" her father asked.

"I think I'll name him Dorian," answered the child. "He looks like a Dorian."

Otis dropped his spectacles back into his smaller pocket. "Meaning Dorian Gray, of course. Oscar Wilde's great age-defying character who bravely turned back the clock of time and met death head on! That is one of your favorite bedtime stories."

"No," said Orphie, more like Dorian Phiddlephart, the night watchman who accidentally fell into one of our open graves and buried himself trying to get out."

"Oh yes. Was he the one with the protruding nose hairs? We never did pull him out."

"At least it gave him a real sense of purpose."

The Goodbyes realized the spider was now quite comfortable with them and had secured itself onto Orphie's scalp like a tightly bound bonnet. Following this, the spider produced a soft veil of yarn-like webbing over Orphie's face.

Pyridine pulled an extra pair of shears from her bag and gave them to Orphie with a chuckle. "I'm confident you'll need those." Orphie began to trim the webbed valance at once.

When Otis was ready to travel, the three piled into the carriage once again. Pyridine took from under her seat a small case. She stuck her head out the window and said to Otis who was driving and Orphie who planted herself on top of the roof with her spider: "If we are going to Nothom, we will need to freshen up on our language - Nothomese." She then opened and unpacked a tiny phonograph and wax cylinder from the case. To make it play, she cranked a small handle on the side. After some slow cranking, the player wound and began to spit out the first sounds of a crackly voice:

"In this lesson, you will learn how Mildred, a person who is conducting surveys, greets Hiram outside his railroad flat. The following questions were asked by Mildred in English and will be followed by their Nothomese translation. We will then track the conversation with Hiram's answers. "Are you ready?" stated the record without pause, "Good, let's begin."

"Afternoon, my name is Mildred. What is yours?"

"Sunobus sunaidirmi, sumus nmoni tsus sitimi. Siuqus tsi

yrtsvus?"

Otis scratched his head, struggling to understand.

"Do you live around here?" the record went on.

"Rorpous sovi ogaus cihrtni?"

"Are you married?"

"Sus sovi muinomirtamus?"

"Do you have any children with four heads?" (Or at least that's what they thought they heard.)

"Rorpous sovi vahus sulli irbilus rpi routtauqus tupaci sitipacus?"

The questioning continued like this for quite some time, until the record ended.

Orphie looked confused. "Can you play that 'Sun-of-a-bus" part again?"

"Right," answered Pyridine. "Back to the beginning, this time, let's try repeating the phrases."

After a moment of more cranking, and perhaps knowing they

sounded not so eloquent, Otis decided to repeat the words in a munchkin-like voice (something he did by pulling his chin into his neck).

"SUnObUs sUnAiDiRmI, sUmUs nMoNi tSuS sItImI. SIuQuS tSi YrTsVuS?"

Orphie and Pyridine laughed and tried themselves, answering in different voices with a few chuckles. The three continued to repeat the first sentence over and over like this until finally giving up and letting the old phonograph spin itself out, while they continued to imitate every squeak and laughed so hard they almost wet themselves.

"That was a close one!" Otis said. "I didn't bring any other pants."

Their laughter was cut short when Orphie heard a popping explosion within what she thought was her eardrum. "Mom, dad! I hear gunfire!??"

"No," Pyridine answered, "that's just your ears adjusting to the underworld."

Chapter X. On the Trail

Meanwhile, not far behind the hearse, Frank Thorne followed the Goodbyes on a stolen horse. Thorne had been tracking the Goodbyes since Otis left Nicklesworth, and the sound of the gunshot that Orphie heard was in fact from his pistol, not her ears popping.

"Dang blasted cave flies," Thorne said having just fired and missed the Giant Borrelia that flew away.

Thorne took back hold of his lantern with the reins in his other hand and pointed the light to the fascinating insects stuck in the webbing around him. The lamp shone brightly off the backs of the Die-Mound Ants. The further Thorne went, the more spectacular the light reflected. The Die-Mound Ants mesmerized Thorne and created an illusion on the canvas tapping into the far reaches of his psyche. The Chthonic he abused in life prevented him from remembering these images that now projected on the canvas like a film. One by one, the images appeared and then dimmed as he passed by. It was a scene of a formal dance, where a man asked for the hand of a beautiful maiden. Thorne was not able to see their faces, only their bodies, and movement. The two bowed and held close, performing a Waltz.

He stopped his horse and removed his rifle cane from its scabbard. He stared intently at the image of the dancers, recalling his past life like a stabbing blade to his heart. "What magic is this, haunting me?"

The memories quickly dimmed.

Thorne grew violent and swatted at the insects with his crooked rifle. The bugs fell from the cut strands of webbing as he bashed at them. But one of the insects, swinging in front of him, and low to the ground, relit and cast a shadow of his past - he was forced to forget. His eyes fixated on the image of the beautiful maiden's face. She held a flower that he recognized he had picked for her at the time. His own fragile memory began to surface, knowing she always wore the flower in her hair to remember him.

He knelt down and set the cane aside.

"M," he stuttered, "Is that you?" Her eyes were motionless, and no words came back, but his own echo. He pulled the Die-Mound Ant from the string. "I am sorry," he said, cradling the bug in his palm. The bug's light soon extinguished, leaving only darkness. He felt an urge to crush it, when no sooner a distraction of voices of the Goodbyes disrupted his thoughts, prompting him to resaddle and go deeper into the underworld.

Chapter XI. Descent

To the relief of Otis, the needlework lifted, and the path was much smoother. The canvas on both sides changed to a glassy black crystal. The faint smell of wolf's bane could be detected as they descended, a noxious odor usually amongst dead things.

"Ah," Otis took a deep luxurious sniff, "You just can't bottle that kind of aroma anywhere."

"We must be getting close," Pyridine assured, lifting a bottle out of her purse and yelling up to Orphie who clung to the carriage roof. "Climb down," she said gruffly. The elixir sized bottle was labeled '100 proof Miasma', made to prevent the skin of the living from sizzling under the fires of Nothom. Orphie joined her mother, climbing through the carriage window and took a seat by her side. "Dab this on," she instructed, mindfully patting the ashy substance over her face and neck before turning it over to the child. She then turned her attention to her husband and asked: "Did you put some on the horse's ears and nose before leaving?"

"Yes, my felch," he replied sincerely.

She took a pinch and sprinkled it over the spider, just in case.

Otis took out a map to confirm their location. "Look's like we are on *tract*," he said.

"Dad, that's not a map that's a man's body," corrected Orphie.

"No, this is a map. One must pass through Nothom to get to the Underworld."

No sooner they saw the amethyst walls reach a clearing. It appeared they had come to the end of the Nothom's pelvis or more specifically the hole of the sacral promontory. Before the Goodbye Family plopped out, they saw a sky twinkling with stars and in-flight ballooned organs of every size. The ground below them wobbled feeling as if they were floating on one such balloon, and after checking, they understood they had. Soon the lower half of the tunnel was fogged with wolf's bane, and Otis shouted out for Midnight to slow. But even still the sensation of galloping maintained.

"Hold on," he choked, placing a handkerchief over his mouth with his free hand. Orphie grabbed her father's hat and waved it back and forth to disperse the rising smoke. Otis yelled for Midnight to brake, "WOAH!" pulling the reins hard. Suddenly, Midnight stopped sharply and the smoke dissipated as they saw they were now heading down the chute. Otis wisely pointed out they were likely traveling through Nothom's large intestine. Twisting around sharp gassy turns that rattled the carriage. The Goodbye Family could feel the intestine begin to move again as their carriage picked up speed toward the rectum, while Otis yelled out to his wife and daughter:

"Prepare for a landing!"

Otis grabbed Pyridine, Pyridine grabbed Orphie, and Orphie caught Dorian the spider perched on her head. A final jolt threw them through two large swinging doors signifying the intestine, had passed the exit and was finally at its end. "So that's what it feels like to be a bowel movement!" said Orphie. Otis's hat having not been securely held on flew off momentarily, but thankfully Pyridine's flying trocar kept it in eyesight and retrieved it quickly soon after.

They had now officially reached the underworld of Nothom. Amidst the twinkling stars above them, the Goodbye family could see a lone gallbladder shaped commuter balloon where several politicians hung by rigs and pulleys with mouths agape blowing hot air into its ascending mouth pipes. They were not gruesome in any way, and the family could tell they were politicians by the banners and pins adorned to their shirts. On the side of the balloon was written "Upon Think", which Otis reminded his daughter was an excellent moral indeed. The words meanwhile duplicated in reverse on its opposite side 'Think Upon' as it passed by.

The parents remembered the sky was once bustling, and that to only see one flying machine was quite unusual. The city was once illuminated with life where bad people fell from the sky

every second and crackled in the Lake of Fire below, and visitors would come and go as they please without restriction and warmly welcomed with a length of a small intestine that they draped around their neck like a Hawaiian lei. But now the Lake of Fire was missing. Nearby the tall rock walls of a mission and a large closed drawbridge prevented anyone from merely entering the city. The tallest vision in the middle of the mission was a stone tower that rocketed skyward into the endless darkness. Neither was it grimly welcoming, but quite dull and uninspiring. At the same time, the nearby amusement park, 'Wits End,' was mostly dismantled. Only rides like the torturous Catherine wheel and the Judas Cradle could be seen outside the rusty and decaying fortress.

"What a terrible mess. What happened down here? Where is our beloved lake?" Pyridine said sadly. The Lake of Fire used to attract many creatures - including the Blister Beetle, but she could only find a small handful of shells which she knew was not the same. They soon wondered if Nothom had indeed become tired and commercial as it was barely recognizable anymore.

The old boardwalk was in its heyday called Boowalk - but was now removed of all it's former splendor. Orphie considered it more of a "Borewalk." The Goodbyes were feeling a heavy weight of sadness, especially Otis who wanted to surprise his wife with his gift and proposal to renew their marriage. *"What is there to rekindle without a flame?"* he thought, unable to see the Lake of Fire. When in an instant, one of Pyridine's rings rattled them from their thoughts:

"Have you landed yet?" The face inside the ring that showed an older woman with an abundance of cat hair in the air, making it look like a tiny snow globe.

"Grandma Yeast," cried Orphie. Looking down at Pyridine's ring.

"It's your mother again," whispered Pyridine to Otis. "It really would be easier if you wore this ring."

"But it was my gift to you," Otis whispered back.

"Yeah, only after your mother gave it to you," she replied.
Grandma Yeast cleared her throat. "Welcome to Nothom. Hope the journey wasn't too rough," she continued in a confidential tone; "Unfortunately as you can tell, Nothom has really gone down the mountain."

"Yes, and how are we supposed to get inside?" asked Otis.

"You have to fill out a contract in advance."

"Contract?" asked Pyridine. "Has it been that long?"

"Four to six lifetimes." answered the grandmother thoughtfully.

"How about four to six cadavers?" replied Otis.

"Not the same," Yeast answered with a laugh, "No four ways about it."

"Don't you mean two?" asked Orphie.

"If I meant two, I would have said so. Always leave yourself a fourth option," Yeast cackled. "You see, to enter, you must go through the mission's gates; then to exit, you must be reborn, and for the locals already," Yeast said with a pause, "you must never have been."

"What is the fourth option?"

"We don't exactly get tourists anymore, outside of those falling in. I'd advise you to take the old road where no one will notice you."

The family waited; mesmerized by her wisdom but concerned

with her logic. "Are you sure you're feeling all right?" asked Pyridine. "I may have some spare arsenic for your head."

"Can't say I rightly know. It's hard to keep myself going with being SAD."

Orphie interrupted, bored of listening to grown-up talk, and knowing her grandmother always had a good story promptly asked: "Can you tell us a story Grandma, please?"

"Don't interrupt, Orphie. Your grandmother was talking," remarked Otis.

"No, that's quite alright. But I can't say I remember many lately." Yeast said in thought. "How about our family creed?"

Orphie replied with an ecstatic, yes, to which Yeast shared the following verse:

But alas this stench,
Why so many tears for digging a grave
That have soiled the depths,
And the eyes still reek.
Freely dissect,
And praise the Goodbye,
Fear yet not,
The rounds of clients
Who waits in a crypt

To hide the ghostly glow
Might a master painted face:
Suffer the nose of flowers,
That long dreary wake
Fields laid soaked in water
The many showers turn to a lake.

The family's claps and cheers came to an abrupt stop when an eerie clanging of chains rang out, and they turned to see in front of the mission the large drawbridge slam down to reveal an entrance. Unexpectedly, out of the darkness, tens of thousands of souls from the recently deceased that the Goodbye Family did not hear or see before sprang up and ran towards the bridge as if attending a great sporting event.

"Mother, we've got to go!" said Otis intending to hang up. "We are going to miss our way in."

"Don't forget to use the old road, it's the safest bet!" Yeast yelled over the distant screams before getting cut off. At this, her happy face tucked back into a blank stare.

They quickly boarded the carriage, and Orphie threw a pickle through the closing doors as Midnight raced up the bridge while the mass of souls crowded behind them.

They entered a holding area between the mission walls and with the drawbridge behind them and iron doors in front. The walls in front of them were several stories higher and contained small windows where they could see faces peering out with rifles. On the ground, the Goodbyes watched as the souls were required to DECLARE any meats, fruits, vegetables, plants, seeds, animals, and plant and animal products or byproducts they may be carrying. This rule included every item they wore or carried, especially anything of value. Some were confiscated, but many of these items were tossed into a large pipe that went downhill to a dark corner of the wall. Most of the souls waited in their knickers and undergarments, two of the bridges split to something of a drop off for newly departed and dearly departed towards a large sign entitled Recruiting Office. Those recently dead were asked to leave the bridge and get into a circle where they were told the shocking news of how they arrived. Seeing how the dearly departed have prepared in advance for such things. An excessively long pat down and prodding took place. They could hear the language seemed to be no longer dominated by Nothomese, but by the same language, the Goodbyes spoke above ground.

"I don't recall any lines like this before," Pyridine said to her husband, "everyone used to just drop in."

Orphie spoke up, "Grandma said something about an old road. Where is that?"

"Ah yes, the old road. The road your mother and I took for our honeymoon." Otis replied in excitement. "Should be around here somewhere." But it was not clearly marked, and the leftover smell of wolf's bane made it impossible for Otis to pinpoint its location. When they were about to call Yeast for directions, they decided instead to follow the pipe that went down a slope and spilled out to a darkened archway in the wall. Their horse stopped short as its hooves locked in the mud.

Otis shone his lantern at the archway that read with faded brickwork "OLD ROAD" verifying they were indeed on the right path but also that it was terribly different. However stuck, he peered down over his seat and being unable to see the ground fully, jumped off the carriage, and splashed his pants in the mud. Pyridine looked out in concern. "What is it?"

"I could have used that second pair of pants after all."

In the dim light, Otis waded knee-deep through the mud trying to pull Midnight forward. There was no budging, and it was soon apparent he was standing in floating trash that slowed their way with bottles, old food, metal parts, broken toys, and the like. Objects that had been collected and brought to Nothom as prized possessions for the souls but worthless to its overseers and quickly discarded into the pipe.

"Everything okay down there?" asked Pyridine, trying to see.

"I'm good," Otis called back, refusing to admit how bad it was. In his effort in freeing the horse's legs, he could feel something wrap around his own legs, grappling them in place and pulling him under.

It was no longer possible to hold back his emotion. "Help!" he cried, "There is a mud-monster pulling me under! This is the end. I know it. I'm doomed. I can feel it. I'm being eaten alive, help!" He gurgled in the mud.

Chapter XII. A Tourist Trap

With all her might, Orphie leaned over the seat and pulled her father easily out of the deep mud. The horse also was able to step back, and the monster revealed itself.

"Looks like a bag of cloth diapers," Orphie reported seeing them float to the surface.

"Yes, but they were super absorbent!" said Otis.

Pyridine shook her head, and Otis lowered his hat over his eyes in embarrassment. A moment passed, and Otis blew the sound of a raspberry and flopped the reins for Midnight to proceed through the mud. They passed under the archway signifying they indeed had found the old road, but it was now being used as the drainage sewer for the mission. Even still, it did not detract the Goodbyes from conjuring a few memories.

"Remember when we first kissed under the stinking corpse flower?" said Pyridine romantically and trying to break her husband's unease.

"How could I forget?" Otis smiled.

"Where exactly was that spot again?" asked Otis, desperately looked around for the flower, thinking it may be the ideal spot to propose once again, but only saw a broken sofa where it once would have been.

The mud shallowed, and Otis had to slick his mustache for several miles; feeling queasy from the mature larger plants along the path that overtook the trail with their roots.

"I have to pee," said Orphie.

"You'll just have to wait," replied Pyridine.

Otis saw an outhouse in the distance. "Look there. We may be in luck."

"Do outhouses always have teeth?" asked Orphie.

Pyridine, who was a master botanist, quickly said through the window, "We'll want to avoid that. It's a carnivorous plant." In fact, the old road had not been traveled on for such a long time that the carnivorous plant had blocked their path, taking the appearance of an outhouse.

The plant had grown so exceptionally impassable that it added a park picnic bench on its opposite side of the road. "Trapis Tourus," she noted, commonly known as a Tourist Trap."

Otis stopped the hearse.

"Father," asked Orphie, "Do you suppose this plant wants to eat us?"

The father turned to her side, "It could," he said with a grin. "But that would put a damper on our trip."

Otis stepped off the wagon to take a closer look.

The shape of the trap at its center had its blades in the appearance of the outhouse door being open and a toilet with hair and teeth, positioned inside, the petiole of the plant. Pyridine knew to take caution getting close since the trap was the mouth of the plant.

Unfortunately, Otis realized the only way they could pass it was

with something it could eat. He stood for a moment in thought. Pyridine called out from the window, "Why not feed it one of our unknown clients?"

"Brilliant idea P," said Otis, reflectively. "We can't raise a dime to bury them. No one will claim them, but the Tourist Trap can."

Orphie climbed off the wagon and unlocked the door for her mother. Pyridine stepped outside, and with the help of her husband, pulled out a body wrapped in a white shroud.

"John Doe, number five," said Otis, looking eagerly at the shroud toward which they drifted. "You don't mind your body being digested over a period of weeks for our benefit, do you?"

The three waited for an answer, but when none came, they unwound number five out of his sheet and held him in their arms. Number five was wearing a golfer's uniform, a hobby he must have been fond of, had a heart attack from, and still had a grip on a polished hickory nine iron.

"Perhaps, we can hold him in a way that he would appear to be moving," declared Pyridine. "Here," said she, "take hold of his feet, and I'll take his hands, and we'll both swing him in the direction of the plant." Pyridine pried the golf club out of number five's hands as they reset their position.

"Okay, stand back Orphie!" announced the father.

Orphie climbed on top of the roof with the club in hand and sat watching curiously while her parents began swinging poor old number five back and forth to build momentum until finally, they said:

"FORE!"

"You mean FIVE!" Orphie replied.

Number five flew towards the plant colliding with a heavy thud. The plant twitched but did not go after the man. Unfortunately, number five landed too far for the plant to properly react.

"Aww banished," said Orphie. "You missed the mark."

"We will just have to trick the plant again." Pyridine chortled.

The parents continued this unsuccessfully between John and Jane Does until at last, they held the final John, also aptly named number two, they brought before the plant.

They decided to creep a little closer this time to set their position and quickly saw that the "toilet" or petiole, mouth part of the plant, was beginning to salivate as they approached. Giving the effect that the toilet was overflowing.

Otis gave a sort of gurgle feeling slightly ill and stopped short, frantically wiping his mustache with his pterodactyl comb three times until he recouped. Resting momentarily, he looked down in the dirt and saw a dollar.

It would have meant very little except for the face upon it, he had remembered from somewhere. "What did you find father?" seeing her father pick up the dollar and bring it to the carriage.
Otis shared it with his wife and child. "I feel like I've seen this man before. Although this dandy looks considerably younger."

Pyridine took the bill and saw the front was a cloaked young man with the increment of one dollar, while the back contained the word Manifest and name Lord Zenwick.

"What's it mean?" implored Orphie.

"Curious and mad," answered Pyridine, "I have no idea what it means. Maybe it's a fraternity slogan of someone named Zenwick."

"A maternity slogan?" asked the child.

"Fraternity," she corrected, giving it back to Otis.

Otis piped up, stirring a memory: "You know when I was a child back east, there was a Zenwick who had all the children in town work his paper route."

"You sold newspapers?" said Orphie with a chuckle.

"No, nothing that dull," replied Otis, "I went house to house like a puppet delivering similar dollar bills with Zenwick's face printed on them, just as this, and the words 'a buck won't save you but Zenwick can."

"How dreadful. Did it at least pay anything?" asked Pyridine astonished.

"Not a thing," he responded, throwing the dollar aside, "But for Zenwick, I suppose. When I tried to cash in these so-called Zenwick bucks, the bankers and mercantile just showed me their own that they had received and warned me of fraud."

"All right," stated Pyridine promptly. "Let's get back to our other leg-pull."

Otis sniffed the air and could smell the plant was opening up by the scent of the John Doe resting so closely, giving him an idea. "Let's park the back of the carriage near the outhouse, to make sure the trap doesn't grab one of us. After that, we'll tie number two up like a puppet. You and Orphie can control his movements from the top of the wagon, clear of the trap, and when the trap sets, I'll back up the horse and wagon through the path."

So to begin, Pyridine took out her crooked needles but soon realized she lacked the necessary thread. She pondered the thought, and after seeing her daughter's unusual veil, inclined to ask: "Orphie, can you see if Dorian can provide us with some webbing." To which the three hoisted number two up to the roof of the wagon, and Orphie brought the spider around number two and watched it swiftly respond with the needed threading for puppet strings. Pyridine stepped up to sew his hands and feet with her needle while Otis proceeded to turn the vehicle around and slowly backed it up, being careful not to dismount the hitch. Pyridine and her child waited until it was in place, before lowering the last John Doe to the front of the thirsty plant. Orphie held the puppet strings like reins on a horse and followed her mother's lead: "Steady," guided P., "Keep your balance. We don't want you to fall in with him."

Otis and Orphie chuckled as Pyridine rolled her eyes watching them dance cadaver number two in front of the trap, providing a sort of enthusiasm to see the outhouse, while Otis imitated his voice: "Oh thank heavens, I have been on the road all day and after eating those nachos could use the toilet!"

The plant's mouth twitched, and Pyridine continued with her instructions, reminding Orphie: "When the trap takes the bait, don't forget to let go."

It was then; the trap lifted its roots off the path and slurped up number two, yanking the puppet strings and Orphie with it, who indeed forgot to let go. Thankfully her new pet Dorian had fastened around her with its webbing and held her down like a seat belt. Orphie let go.

Knock, Crash! Burp! Went the outhouse, and it made so much

clatter digesting number two that they were much more terrified that it might regurgitate him so they flattened themselves out onto the wagon and Otis turned around the carriage in a rush and fled past the plant.

"Haha - and we're off!"

Chapter XIII. Thorne Recollects

A short distance behind, Frank Thorne also had to dismount his horse and pull his horse carefully through the garbage that spilled out from the pipe.

"DANG GUMMIT!"

Thorne was a seasoned horseman and knew it was not possible to simply pull his horse out of the mud by the neck, legs or tail. Instead, he took the whip out of his satchel and harnessed it around the barrel or underside of the horse. Yet, Thorne faltered and tugged on the horse with all his strength, but the horse would still not move.

"COME ON BUZZARD BAIT!" he yelled. "I'll make you move if it's the last thing I do."

Again Thorne yanked on the horse violently as it neighed back. The outlaw's hands slipped from the reins, landing him backward in the mud.

SPLASH!

"BLAM JAM!" he cried, proceeding to throw mud in every

direction.

He pounded his fists in the mud, and after a dozen punches, he tapped on something sharp and buried. A nail stuck to his hand and unknowingly he pulled out a broken picture frame. Curiously, he wiped the mud off with his sleeve. It had been damaged on one side showing only the dancer everyone knew as Emma Blu. It must have been a wedding photo for it showed her in an innocent white gown.

Suddenly, Thorne felt a stabbing pain in his chest and thought for a moment he had been shot in the heart.

"Great mountain!" he choked, freezing stiff in place.

He tried turning his body to see if there was a shooter, but another jolt struck him, crippling him to his knees.

Thorne nearly blacked out, crashing into the mud atop the frame.

SPLAT!

His face rested eye to eye with Emma Blu staring back at him in the photo.

Chapter XIV. Bridge of Sighs

After a good deal of complaints from Orphie, the Goodbyes path crossed an old bent street sign marked 'The Highway of Bones,' and came to a ruined bridge, once called the Bridge of Sighs. The bridge was in disrepair and consisted mostly of tall deformed statues, many of which were missing digits, limbs, and heads.

"You know," said Pyridine pointing out the sign to her daughter, "This used to be the Lover's Lane of Nothom."

They were beginning to feel a little uneasy until Otis smelled the faint aroma of barbecue skewered Hog Frog, a typical treat sold by vendors of Nothom. "Do you smell that?" he said with renewed hype.

"Yes, I think Orphie relieved herself off the carriage roof," said Pyridine.

"No, not that!" He replied, picking up speed moving around the fallen blocks as each remaining statue above animatedly turned to look down at them. Otis abruptly stopped the hearse at a rusty iron gate portioned between the mission walls. They could tell the city rerouted the sewage down the sloped trail. On the gate, it used to read 'Memento Mori' but sadly, the letters 'me' in the middle of

'Memento' had fallen off, and the 'M' in 'Mori' was now dangling upside down, leaving it to read 'Mento Wori.'

"That's Latin for 'Remember you must worry,'" Otis instructed to his daughter. "In case you should forget."

An unusual statue stood above the gate on top of a wall, tipped over in a seating posture and raising its arm as if it had grappled something before.

Otis jumped off the carriage and tried to open the locked gate.

The strange figure sitting above them decided to speak. "That's a crime, you know."

Otis turned around to his wife, "What did you say my armoire?" Otis's way of saying Mi Amor.

"It was the statue," she said with interest. "It spoke."

"Oh yes," said Otis, now observing the statue more carefully. I forgot they do that here."

The sculpture sighed, "There is nothing for us anymore. No one recognizes us. Only that we are made of stone."
"I won't "quarry" with you about that," returned Otis, looking at it with big eyes.

The figure twisted its head and exclaimed: "I bet you don't even know who I am."

The three thought for a moment. Otis sat down and watched his daughter, who was cutting more webbing from her veil the spider had produced. "I got it," Otis announced clicking his fingers, "Sam Lucas, the actor!"

The figure shook its head despairingly.

"Hardly a male minstrel," Pyridine corrected through the window, "has a chin like Pauline Musters. Or at least I hope you might be Pauline. I've been dying to meet you. But you seem taller than 23 inches. Still, with your slouch, you could be."

"I beg your pardon?" cried the statue, willfully tipping further.

"Are you Mayet?" suggested Orphie. "The Goddess who weighs us?"

"Sorry, but not even close," remarked the sculpture, in a tone of defeat, "she's further down the road without a head."

"No wonder no one takes the highway anymore." Mumbled Pyridine to her child. Soon after, Otis popped up from his seat and said with a shriek, "No wait, I know it! I know it!"

"Yes?" retorted the statue, more directly, "Yes?" it leaned in, now face to face with Otis.

"Teddy Bilbo, the lunatic!"

"No," commanded the sculpture, with an angry flash of her fading eyes, "if I had my scepter, I would stab you."

Otis looked at his wife and shrugged.

"Whatever happened to the times when people used to hold festivals in our honor?" the statue replied, catching Otis by the arm. "When people would give their last piece of bread for us?" It sunk further, releasing him from its grip, "Have we grown so weak that no one remembers us?"

"You are a bit of a slouch." Otis pointed out. "Have you tested for osteoporosis?"

"I would not doubt that." cried the statue, struggling frantically to stretch itself back up, "I guess I have lost all my mineral wealth after all." The figure continued to sulk, while Otis sensibly pulled out his skeleton keys to test them on the gate.
"That will never work," it called down. "Unless you have a membership?"

"Can't say we do," Otis grunted, "Are you reciprocal with CHMA or the funerary director's guild?"

"No, not anymore," it said drawing back. "You could try knocking three times."

Otis rattled his knuckles painfully against the gate.

"But that won't work either," answered the stone creature in a meek voice. "It was silly of me to suggest."

"Ghastly creature!" said Pyridine, "And no wonder the sewage drains here, you are certainly full of it."

"Hmph," the figure drooped. "Unfortunately, seeing how this is now a high-class establishment, I am not supposed to let just any unworthy souls such as yourselves walk in. Particularly those who take the short cut through the sewer."

"Not even if we take pride in being unworthy?" said Otis truthfully. "Surely, that has to account for something."

The statue stared crossly at the family. "If you knew my name, you would obviously know a password."

"Go on then, we won't wear it out."

"You have three minds, a horse, and a spider," Snapped the statue. "Put them to work!"

"And we will have a hearse full of mag-flies too if we have to wait very long," demanded Pyridine.

"Waiting is my specialty. At least I have plenty of that." The statue said, turning slightly away. It was momentarily quiet, as the sculpture peeked to see if they may have left, but as they had not, it said with a hint: "I also am good at sowing. Do you like to sow?"

"Certainly," said Pyridine, "sewing is one of my specialties."

"What do you reap," asked the statue, believing she was speaking of sowing a garden, "is it radishes, celery, or olives?"

"Not usually, unless they were in somebody's stomach at the time of death."

As the two discussed sowing, or what they believed to be the topic, Otis thought if he were to send his hat over the wall, that somehow, between the hat and the flying trocar looking to retrieve it, that they could find a way to unlock the gate from the other side. It was downright a terrible idea, but much to the discredit of Otis, he threw his hat in the air, and the statue which had dropped so low and weak, was smacked by the hat, and shattered before Otis's feet.

CRASH! CRUMBLE!

They were motionless for a time, and then Pyridine who actually enjoyed the conversation, oblivious to the mix up of sowing and sewing, let out an awful gasp.

Otis felt horrible but was at a complete loss for words. His mouth quivered searching for the right thing to say. "Oops!"

At this, the iron doors flung freely open, and Pyridine who was briefly distracted from scolding Otis, watched as he picked up his hat and the three anticipated what was behind the door.

"I guess that was the password," Orphie shrugged.

A moment later, behind them, Frank Thorne rode through the gate and advanced directly to the tower.

Chapter XV. More Disappointment

In a short distance, Otis and his family came to a large sign where it once read Deadfalls but was now crossed off with the words written underneath 'It's good to be alive in Nothom.'

Walking ahead, they were startled by how much the town around them had changed. The area once had a carnival atmosphere, where peddlers sold their wares under weeping willows or draped their bargains over gravestones. Now, it was the home of a hotel called the Posy Palace and whatever few businesses that remained were purposely being sabotaged by the new owner of the neighboring mega-store called Mission Mart. Only a few old stores were holding on dotted beside shrubs made from human hair, twisting and curling with delicate precision around a wire. Crowds of souls went about their business, mindlessly bumping and brushing past the Goodbyes.

"This is truly the last of it," said Pyridine to Orphie. "This street once had B-Ware Photograph, where tourists could take photos with monsters before they were eaten, a scratchy phonograph store for the insane called Chris' Demented. And further afield was the Cavity (literally a hole in a giant's tooth that acted as a playground for smaller souls), Mindwave the demonic fortune teller, and Barbed Wire Habit a clothing shop that cut off your circulation.

Jugglers used to travel freely on unicycles, mimes were miming, and even ventriloquists making pleasant conversation with themselves."

The only thing of delight to the Goodbyes was a sorry looking skeleton locked in a shrew's fiddle atop a weeping willow they called Jack.

"Looks like Jack is all that's left," Otis sighed.

"And that's not much of him," replied Orphie. "He's a fixture that's for sure." The skeleton was missing his feet, and the fiddle was tied with the fragile veins from his arm and played with a bow made of his bone and hair. It played as every fiddle from the world above, and along with the neck violin, it was once the favorite instrument below as it produced the most mournfully sweet sounds. Now it was only a relic.

Otis parked the funeral carriage under a frizzled fro-bush and jumped off. He tied Midnight to this, while Orphie with the tarantula in her hair climbed down to the ground to unlatch the back door for her mother. Pyridine retied the rattails around Otis's finger, and the three half-heartedly investigated the remaining shops. At first, all was gray and agreeable, but when they turned around a mausoleum, they were blinded by a row of newly painted condominiums drooping red crepe paper between their doors with dead Giant Borealis attached like flypaper. Chimes dangled beside their doorways and planters of ivy hung down from their rooftops onto those passing by below.

"A real disgrace," Otis said, picking the crab apple head off one Borealis.

"Yes, whatever happened to the rusty chimes and planters of drooping hemlock?" Pyridine frowned.

Otis started chewing it as he tried to reply, but none could understand him with his mouth full.

"All these changes," Pyridine gasped. "My body can't handle it." She sat momentarily feeling faint.

Orphie was also getting tired and bored, as the souls went about their business around them.

"It's not all so bad," Otis said. "Look at these poor souls. Never saw a sadder lot. At least we are not so selfish." It was a careless thing to say and not his best attempt at humor. Otis felt he was failing, perhaps as a husband or father and decided, a bit unwisely it was the right time in the middle of the crowd of people, for it couldn't get worse, to get on one knee and propose his love again to Pyridine under the sign.

"My bat," said Otis beginning with salty eyes, taking her hand, "I have something to say."

"Do you mean to vomit?"

"No," Otis shook his head. Orphie looked on curiously while the souls continued brushing against them. Orphie had to part the souls between her parents, to give them space, but the souls grew louder with ghostly groans and moans and pressed them closer. "Otis, can't this wait?" Pyridine said in a nervous interest.

"We've been together since your first spell," Otis continued, he said under the roar of groans and moans, "and years could not separate us," he stumbled from being pushed over, "consider," he continued...

"I can't hear you," said Pyridine, "all this noise."

Before he could finish, Otis and Pyridine's hand released and Orphie could not hold back the tide of souls any longer as the party was swept up and carried into the town square. Otis saw Pyridine float off in the wave of souls.

After a few minutes, they washed ashore on top of a mausoleum and brushed themselves off of all the ghostly dust that passed by. The souls dispersed, and Pyridine had the mind to ask: "What were you asking?"

But Otis felt pure defeat. "I will tell you later."

They climbed down from the mausoleum and found themselves

in front of a small crypt selling faded mourning attire with a sign above the tomb reading 'Magasin de Deuil.' A sign on the door read 'Customers Wanted.'

"Sounds like a couture shop," Otis remarked. "Let's see if they can help."

Otis opened the creaky door as dust sprinkled down on them. "Hello?" he announced, seeing layers of soot over the merchandise. Inside the store, there were twelve individuals shopping. Otis led his family to the first few asking each about the bookstore. But upon approaching, he quickly realized that they were, in fact, the shop's mannequins posed to look as if they were shopping. In the back of the store, and hiding, they found another that seemed to be a young girl. On closer inspection, it was a child-sized mole with a black wig over her face and wearing a black bonnet and a funeral gown. She sat atop a high stool, looking down at a book.

"Excuse me," said Otis, "Do you know where I might find the Baron's son?"

She looked up from her book and turned towards Otis. "This is not my name, Baron, nor," she added hostilely, "am I a son."

She began reading aloud. "Be careful in conversation to avoid topics which may be supposed to have any direct reference to events or circumstances which may be painful for your companion

to hear discussed."

"Of course," replied Otis. "Good point. But do you know where I might find him?"

"I don't know, and I don't care," replied the mole.

Orphie saw she was reading a book entitled '*Principles of Good Taste*,' and having more interest in finding creepy things interrupted: "Do you know where I might find a creepy book?"

The mole stopped reading and placed a dusty marker into the book, lowering it to her lap with attitude. "I am not creepy." She said with a breathy air. "If you can see, you would have seen I'm also busy reading. If you were listening, you would have noticed I am not interested in your questions. If you were aware of your surroundings, you would see there are plenty of other people to help you," pointing to the mannequins, "and just to speed things up, if you were shopping, all dresses are 2 for 1." She lowered her head back into reading the book.

"Who wears two dresses at once?" replied Orphie.

Pyridine leaned forward with her longest fingernail and brought the mole's pointy nose to her hand, gazing assertively at its eyes. "We were not asking WHO you are, what YOU are doing, where YOU'RE from, what's ON sale, or if YOU were creepy. My husband was asking you about the Baron's son while my daughter was just asking for creepy things." Pyridine took the book from the mole's lap and scratched the page before her cutting it into two.

The mole girl mumbled, pointing with an outstretched claw: "Maybe my boss knows." Before climbing off into the dusty hanging shirts above.

So the family walked themselves to the front counter where they slid past the vacuous shoppers until reaching the boss who was a ninety-year-old giant snake holding an ear trumpet.

"Do you know where I might find the Baron's son?" asked Otis to the old snake. "We have a delivery."

"I can't say I've heard anything," he hissed, placing the horn mistakenly at every corner of its head.

"Maybe you are holding it wrong?" Pyridine moved the horn closer to what she imagined to be its ear.

"Not if I was trying to smell you," said the old snake sticking out its tongue.

"Do you know where I can find a creepy book?" asked Orphie.

Unfortunately, the owner proceeded to tell them about the "boots" upstairs, which the family tried to explain it was "book" not "boot" that their daughter was interested in, but that did not seem to matter, and after a short debate, they gave up and left the store.

The only other business in view was another block down, a library called the "Antiquarium Society," where a pocket of recently deceased gathered at its front door.

"Not the best at spelling," Otis said noting the antiquarium rather than antiquarian. Nevertheless, Orphie pulled them towards the library, with the strength of an elephant, plowing through the crowd to get inside.

Chapter XVI. The Antiquarium Library

The library was made to look like a sunken pirate boat cut in half and its captain's quarters, or that is the captain cut into quarters hung on the wall. The family feeling that time was ticking decided to split up. Otis approached a strange creature behind the information desk, who had the head of a cavefish and wore two cockleshells for eyeglasses, while Pyridine perused behind him for the Witches quarterly. Orphie continued her search for creepy things.

"Excuse me." Otis began, "I am looking for the Baron's son. Any idea where I can find him?"

"The Baron's son, you say?" the librarian answered, looking away from Otis. "You've come to the right place," she said handing over the same book the girl in the store was reading, *Principles of Good Taste*."

"Where?" asked Otis looking down and back up again.

"Here." She presented yet another copy of the book *Principles of Good Taste*.

Otis looked confused.

"He is everywhere," the librarian said pointing around the room for *Principles of Good Taste*. "The Baron's son was the test case for our beautifully crafted etiquette book *Principles of Good Taste* by Lord Zenwick."

"Test case?" Pyridine inquired, "Didn't know he was also dead."

"This library's no good at all!" cried Orphie. "They've only got one book."

"But look at how many sizes and colors it comes in," answered the librarian.

It was soon apparent to Otis and Pyridine the library was nothing but *Principles of Good Taste* in various editions and sizes. There was even a section of used, miniature and children's copies.

Pyridine flipped through the pages of the book and came to a chart detailing step-by-step of how the sinners of the underworld (or cinders as they are named locally) are given transport into the living by having their essence sucked up and bottled in the tonic. Pyridine read aloud, "When a person above ground drinks the tonic, the essence is put into their bloodstream. If the person should die with it in their bloodstream, the essence then takes over the body and becomes its new host."

Meanwhile, Orphie's attention was stolen from the inspecting adults when she thought she saw a small sapling creep across the hall.

"This could be creepy!" Orphie grinned and tiptoed to the dark corner where the plant was hiding.

On closer inspection, she saw a small boy who was made entirely out of grass twisted together to form its head, body, and appendages. He stood no more than an inch high with scraggly hair. She watched him curiously as he began ripping pages with his teeth out of a book on the bottom shelf of an aisle.

The girl's pursuit was interrupted by a scowling cave salamander in a shawl. "Have you picked up your copy of *Principles of Good Taste*," he said, pressing the book into Orphie's chest.

"No thanks," Orphie replied, dodging around the librarian, pushing him out of the way. "I find the topic rather murky."

"This one is quite undulating. You should consider picking yourself up a copy. Every little monster is doing so."

"Thank you, but I am not a monster," Orphie declared matter-of-factly. "I am a Goodbye." She scanned the back shelves for the grass boy, who she spied sneaking toward the exit with the pages he tore.

"I assure you, it is luring," the librarian pressed on. The salamander blocked Orphie's path again. "Who always stands in line, is articulate, in fashion, but never borrows?"

"A thief made of grass?" asked Orphie.

"It was a question, that's why I asked."

Orphie attempted to follow the tiny boy. But in this action, she riled the librarian to say. "What is it you are exactly looking for then? Besides stealing!"

"I am not the one stealing?"

"Yes you are, you are stealing my breath," the salamander said in shock. "You certainly do not deserve to be called a monster."

"Security! Security!" The salamander screamed in panic.

A second cavefish that stood upright on his two tails for feet scuttled towards her. "Stop!" he yelled.

Orphie did not curtail her freakish strength when she lost her patience and shoved the salamander back against a bookshelf. The impact caused a domino effect and row after row of copies of *Principles of Good Taste* came crashing down. She ran towards the door, passing by her father and mother who were looking confused all at the same time. "I'll be right back," she said aloud. To which they turned slightly thinking they heard someone or something but weren't entirely clear on who or what it was?

It did not take long for the twisted grass boy to realize Orphie was on his tail, quite literally, as she was stepping on a piece of him that unwound from his body. She tripped, but the wind against her hair was blowing the spider off her scalp. It left and dragged a vast web behind her leading back to the library. Thankfully the webbing also made a useful net for it entangled the cave fish to stop. The grass boy meanwhile hobbled on one foot around a corner of an obelisk and jumped out of sight.

Chapter XVII. Fleck

Orphie crouched, making as little noise as possible. She saw a giant tipped over Tear Jar (also called a Weeping Vase) and the small green sprig poking out to see her. She had seen the jar before when it was used to collect mourners tears that could then be buried with their loved ones.

The Tear Jar was plastered together in pieces of books. There was a miniature chair of hardbound pages; a table of encyclopedia pages and a dresser of bookmarks. Her fascination grew: "Is this your home?" she asked.

The small twisted grass boy timidly cowered under his bed made from a folded book cover.

"My name is Orphie," she coaxed. "You don't have to be scared."

Orphie noticed most of the room was a collection of torn out pages of '*Principles of Good Taste*,' but commented instead on a small hollow quill pen which she mistook for a musical instrument. "Do you like to play that horn?"

The boy remained silent under the bed and revealed the ripped apart pieces of the pages he stole.

"I play a tuba myself," she continued. "It's like yours, but longer, serpent-shaped. It goes bwaaa, bwaaa, bwaaa. I play it at home all the time." Orphie mimicked the sound blowing into her hand until the boy interrupted.

"You know you have a spider in your hair?" he said.

"Oh yes! I nearly forgot. I should have introduced you sooner. My spider's name is Dorian. It is a special Needlework Tarantula."

"Won't he make your hair knotty?"

"Yes, very naughty, but that's okay by me." Hey, you can speak!" Orphie said with excitement.

"Of course. I know all the languages of those down here."

"I do not live here; we are just visiting," Orphie replied, curiously looking out over his room. "But it has been an awful vacation."

"Good, there are too many of you already."

"Really?! I've only met one of me!"

"You know what I mean," he said brushing it off. "People like you."

"No one is like me. I am a Goodbye."

Orphie gave the torn piece of his body back to Fleck. "I'm very sorry about stepping on you." She replied sorrowfully. The grass boy tried putting the part back on like a shoe, but it would not stick.

"If only I had some glue," she suggested seeing his dilemma. It was then Dorian, the Needlework Tarantula, climbed down from Orphie's hair and offered his sticky spider webbing to "clot" the boy's wound. With an application, it stuck the two pieces back together and lifted the poor boy's spirit.

Orphie then spied a folded dollar bill that was currently being used as a blanket for his bed. "Where did you get your blanket?" She asked thoughtfully.

"I have a lot in a pile outside," he answered. "They are Zenwick bucks, it's the currency around here."

"Wow, my father told me of those. May I have one?" said Orphie, placing her finger back into the Weeping Vial.

"Sure, but I don't see how it will help. It's completely wrong and not to scale."

The grass boy suddenly recognized Orphie's enormous size before him and crouched back.

Orphie could see Fleck was distraught. She reached into the Tear Jar with her finger to gently brush his scraggly hair. Unfortunately, upon doing so, she felt a slight papercut but continued to remain calm as if nothing had happened: "It's been a terrible vacation. I can't wait to get home."

Fleck made no reply but dropped his head in sadness and cried. Tears of ink dripped down his face and puddled to the floor. "I wish I still had my town and people like me around," he shuddered.

Orphie had a clever idea and took the bill from his bed, avoiding sticking her hand in the puddle of ink. "Do you have scissors?" she inquired.

"I just rip my pages out," Fleck said trying to tear it. But the Zenwick bill was too thick for his tiny hands.

"No, no. Let me try." Orphie attempted to rip it and felt the weight of her mother's extra shears in her pocket. She took them out and showed Fleck how to make a paper doll chain matching his height.

She took the remaining folded bill and folded it again into quarter's accordion style. She did not have a pencil but tried her best to gauge a character based on the boy with his arms extended beyond the edge of the folded sheet. She gave the cut bill to the twisted grass boy and told him to open it. When he did, they could see three identical Flecks linked hand-in-hand.

The boy was full of excitement. "Oh, you have given it life!"

"You'll have to find a pencil to draw their eyes, ears, and a mouth and they'll be just like you. Except they won't be able to talk, see, or listen." Orphie clipped the paper Fleck's apart to free them from the bill.

"Not true," He exclaimed, "I just need to assign each a preface. It's our way in Unabridged."

With this, he took the quill pen and dipped it into his own puddle of tears which Orphie figured the secretion must have been similar to Blister Beetle Sweat, for after all, she brought to life her mother's flying trocar and her father's hat the same way. Orphie watched as he opened and dipped the quill into the bottle and began brushing the paper figures as he said the following:

Blot,
chalk,
foolscap,
nib,
felt,
slip.

It really must have been magic for as he spoke and held each of their hands, the lines formed in the following order giving them each eyes, a mouth, hair, nose, ears, gender and a most importantly a brain to do what they could not otherwise do. Orphie could see their brains grow through the paper, translucent at first like the shell of a new bug, but in moments they hardened and could not be seen. "What they lack now will grow in time," said Fleck.

"What did all that mean?"

"Activate light in the body, and illuminate."

"Fascinating," exclaimed Orphie, astonished. "You can have these shears." she went on. "I can get another pair."

"Thank you; these will come in handy. Do you mind taking a moment to name these three?"

"By all means," she said, as he retreated to fold and cut out more. The three paper people looked on in anticipation. There was one who looked more like a woman, so she named her; "Bess," and one who appeared to be a man she thought "Leroy," while the third was gender neutral, she called "Lou."

The boy stepped out from under the bed and examined her intensely. He could see she was quite different from the souls who wandered about, most of whom would never dream of wearing a tarantula on their heads. "My name is Fleck." He presented a sorrowful welcome by swooping the bangs out of Orphie's eyelashes like turning the pages of a book.

"What an impressive greeting," Orphie said.

"People used to drop in from the sky all the time. I believe your land had a name for them?"

"Sinners?"

"No, no, cinders." He continued anxiously. "They were called 'cinders' because of how nicely they fell directly into the Lake of Fire. The nasty ones were punished for eternity in our old amusement park Wits End. Sadly, ever since Lord Zenwick took over, he closed both and the cinders no longer magically fall, but are safely redirected to become citizens of Nothom."

"Citizens? That sounds terrible. Who is this Zenwick?"
Fleck sat down, feeling distraught. "According to the etiquette book, Zenwick is the supreme ruler of Nothom and helped build the Baron's army to create harmony in the world above. It boasts

he is a great wizard that found the secret to immortality, but I know the truth. I've seen what he has done to our grass people." Fleck paused. "What is a paper man if he has not been granted a conditional pardon, is he not a document of his own proof?"

"What do you mean, what he has done?"

Fleck perused his room for the answer from the pages of *Principles of Good Taste*. "The book talks about Zenwick meeting the Baron's son, but his name is not mentioned in the book. At first, the son was not business minded like his father." He stopped momentarily from reading to look sternly at Orphie. "It is a rumor here, but I've heard he wanted to help people." He rushed to the far corner of the room to look at another ripped passage. "The son was on his father's mining expedition and struck a geyser of oil. He found the oil could be bottled as a powerful elixir for anxiety to paralyze emotion." He ripped a piece off the ceiling and turned to Orphie and sat crisscrossed, continuing to read: "The son went to his father with the elixir, but the Baron at first did not see its promise. Fleck stepped off his bed. "This means, he didn't see any financial reward. I have found the rest of the book to be lies. I heard the Baron disowned his son after that, and left him broke and destitute. It was only after the son began overusing the elixir on himself that Zenwick entered the picture and sort of took over."

"Did anyone stop him?"

Fleck paused, reflecting on the ripped off piece of his body. "He is a powerful wizard. We are so delicate, to say the least." the boy said to Orphie, "Besides I could never reach the tower where he lives. Every day his army gets bigger as more cinders sweep in. I suppose a few locals got away, but many were destroyed while others became his servants. I just hope I can bring the town of Abridge back."

"Is that the name of this place?" asked Orphie.

"No, it was Unabridged." Returned Fleck, "But I would settle for the people from Abridge."

Orphie lied down to peer into the bottle more comfortably. "Why was the library filled with only books on *Principles of Good Taste*?"

"His guidebook is the only book allowed here. He promises those who follow him will live again above ground," said Fleck softly; and then paused for a moment, as if in thought. Finally, he said: "Not to mention, some of the cinders, who are full of gas, easily leak back up into your world through the pumps and invade the bodies of the paralyzed."

"Is that why the cinders no longer fall from the sky? So they can repopulate the earth above?"

"Yes, and it's all his fault."

"Sounds like he really shook things up."

Orphie turned to look at the sky.

Fleck took a strip of binding and laid it down at the front of his door as he walked out. He wiped his feet and pointed: "See those ghastly bright stars? It is only a theory, but I believe that people go up to those stars when they are turned. We did not have them before. I think the star is bright because we see your world through it."

Orphie looked at the boy in wonder. "But why would the cinders go up?"

"Gas can only go up in a world below."

"Speaking of this world," the tiny thankful boy said: "I have a lot of work cut out to do. I hope the next time I see you, our town will thrive once more."

"Abridge."

"Yes, Abridge. A new start!" He exclaimed, "You will always be welcome."

Orphie placed Dorian into her pocket and heard in the distance her parents calling while Fleck prepared to introduce a new set of paper friends to Bess, Leroy, and Lou.

Blot,
chalk,
foolscap,
nib,
felt,
slip.

Chapter XVIII. Movin' on Up

"Oh, there you are!" said Pyridine, "Where have you been?"

"My friend Fleck lives down the trail."

"He lives in a litter box?"

"No, no," Orphie corrected and directed their eyes to the Tear Jar. "He resides in Unabridged. Lord Zenwick decimated their grass town."

Pyridine bent down and collected a sample of the ground into a flask.

"I don't suppose he knows where we can find the Baron's son?"

"Sounds like he may live in the tower with Zenwick?"

"Sounds like two dingbats in the belfry." Pyridine said as they gazed at the tower in the distance.

They could not see its top for it vanished into the darkness above, while below thirteen beastly guards posted inside thirteen vertical windows and thirteen wretched soldiers stood in front of the tower door on the ground.

They walked toward the tower door, seeing it heavily guarded - and the only way up seemed to be an impossibly dangerous path. They braced themselves and started, but the hat and trocar knew better - and pulled in the opposite direction.

"Settle down, you two," she scolded. "Must I always have to separate you!" Pyridine and Otis grab their flying accessories to separate them, but the trocar angrily lifted Pyridine into the air while Otis also rocketed upwards with his hat. Thankfully, Orphie took hold of Otis just in time as they hitched a ride upwards.

The guards below raised their guns, but it was too high and not soon enough. They fired with missed shots. A lone guard in the highest window was peaking out when he saw the three rocket towards him. "Get out of the way!" screamed Pyridine.

Chapter XIX. The Mission

The three yelled as the trocar and hat torpedoed the Goodbyes into the tower's highest window where a guard peered out.

CRASH!

It was a perfect hit, blasting and flattening the guard! The impact dislodged their pockets, spreading their belongings across the floor. Otis concentrated on picking up his pickles and tools while Pyridine helped gather his things and Orphie scrambled for a way out. She could see a spiral staircase with lanterns lighting the way and realized it was not really a tower they were in but a type of well, with rope and bucket at its center.

There was very little time as the guards on the other floors were quickly ascending the stairs. "We seem to be intact," said Pyridine looking over them and putting the trocar away. "Did you really have to be so hasty?" Pyridine reprimanded her embalming rod.

Otis returned his hat to his head. "So sensitive they are."

"Let's get this over with!" shouted Orphie, who was becoming quite perturbed with the whole trip.

Thankfully they were near the top and climbed up a ladder that led to the top of the well. After a moment, the Goodbyes fell out over the brim of the portal exhausted. They had made it above ground but were now in the middle of an oil refinery where workers went about pumping oil. The loud drilling prevented the Goodbyes from being heard and anyone being able to communicate with them. Pyridine's ring shook. Yeast shouted: "What's taking you so long?" Pyridine held her breath, cautious not to make a sound.

"We've been a little-sidetracked," Otis yelled to the ring to be heard. "We will need to call you back."

"What?" Yeast sounded angry as screeching cats were all around her. "No," she said, "you are going to talk to me right this second."

Pyridine glared at Otis, warning him to silence the cantankerous cat lady. "If we get caught, we'll never be able to leave this place. I'll be stuck with my mother-in-law and her cats for eternity, and you!" Her eyes narrowed, "You'll be stuck with me."
Otis gulped. "What is it, mother?" he whispered.

"What?"

"I said, what is it?"

"Since you did not stop over, I have gone ahead and made arrangements for us to convene at the Posy Palace in Nothom."

"We were planning on seeing you before the rainstorm," Otis began.

"But, there is no time for a stopover now," Pyridine cut off. "More pressing matters have arisen. You must understand."

"I guess you don't want to see me," Yeast appeared sulking. "So easy to forget your relatives when you're frolicking on holiday." The oil drilling continued at a loud volume.

"We can see you on the way back," Otis guiltily conceded. "We can have a bite to eat together. But outside of that, there's just no time."

One by one, the rings began to glow and shake with the cries of their undead relatives; their ghastly faces guilt-tripping the Goodbyes with pouts and sobs.

"No, no. Stop. We had our hearts set on seeing you and the Lake of Fire before returning."

"You don't love me anymore." Yeast mumbled, between all the rings other tears.

"That is not true," Otis spoke directly into Pyridine's ring finger, looking back at her. "We love you as much as a poison sumac bath."

"Stop it, mom! Stop it, dad." scolded Orphie. "You are making Grandma cry." Otis and Pyridine looked at each other in defeat.

"Now say sorry," Orphie said with her fists placed on her hips.

"We are sorry, mother."

"Does that mean you will stay over?"

"Fine," Pyridine sighed heavily. Yeast suddenly stopped crying along with the rest of the family of rings and continued as if it had never happened. "So as I was saying, I've booked the Posy Palace..."

"Posy Palace." They groaned.

"Yes, it's another one of those changes done to attract tourists; it's the only hotel in town that had enough rooms."

"Enough rooms. What do you mean?"

"I've taken liberties to reserve enough rooms for all of our family to be there." To which the handful of rings cheered shaking Pyridine's hands.

"You shouldn't have gone to all this trouble."

"Fine. Witching hour it is.'

"Tomorrow at twelve o'clock? How are we going to manage that?" exclaimed Otis.

"You are not allowed to be late," said Yeast. "Haven't you done enough to your poor mother?"

To which Orphie again asked for their apology.

"We are sorry mother."

"You cannot hide from a Goodbye." Shrieked Yeast.

The worried family stopped talking as Frank Thorne and several guards heard their chatter and with their guns pointing at them directed: "We are expecting you."

Chapter XX. Disaster Pastor

Otis shrieked at the sight of Thorne. "It's you again?"

"Thank you for showing me the way," Thorne said coldly.

The guards searched the family, and after a tediously long wait piling up their hacksaws, scissors, needles, medical equipment, and one shrunken head. Otis was perplexed they had not found the Chromus Humbug in his pocket. "*I must have lost it.*" he gravely thought and said aloud: "We have to go back! There is something very important, I must find." But Thorne and the guards ignored his pleas and marched them to the mission marked 23 Skidoo Street. Here, they saw many of the old pieces from the early Nothom days now dressing the outer archway of the mission. One statue was a large potato with the words "*Potatoe*" carved into its side, misspelled on purpose.

"Tasteless." Pyridine said pointing it out to her husband.

"Seedy art to put it mildly," Orphie added. "Such a pithy."

Otis remained silent thinking about the lost gift for Pyridine.

The mother who was technically on hold, was now released and replied: "What did you say? I am not vexatious."

"No, Yeast. We are not speaking of you," replied Pyridine.

"I certainly hope not. I may be seedy, but I am not vexatious."

Thorne hobbled in lead to the mission door. "Zenwick doesn't like kids," he said brushing away Orphie. "You'll have to wait outside."

Orphie shrugged her shoulders and replied: "Fine, I don't like him either."

Thorne took Orphie by the neck with the crook of his cane. "What did you say, child?"

"I said, I don't like him. I don't like you, and I haven't liked this vacation!" Orphie stomped.

"My, my, little bat do calm down. There is no need to get worked up." Pyridine insisted gently removing Thorne away from her daughter. "Do apologize to this man."

"Aww banished! I will not."

"Please accept my apologies." Pyridine said to Thorne, "We are not having the best go of things. We don't want to cause any trouble. We are here to do business."

"Fine, I'll go easy on her; she's just a kid, anyhow."

"Oh, my goth," Pyridine said under her breath. "I mean, you don't want to upset HER." She raised her voice. "Now do try and be civil. Orphie, my bat, do kindly wait outside."

Chapter XXI. Cata-Chthonic

The family entered the hall of the mission. It had a large dome roof with a giant wheel at the center and gears and pipes extending off of it. From out of the steam, a finely dressed young man approached the Goodbyes. He had long blonde hair and a necklace with a large Z on it. He stood at the center of the room with caskets built into the walls around him. In bold print on one of the caskets nearest the Goodbyes read "Mother" while on the opposite side of the room, the upright coffin read "Father." The casket window for the mother's side revealed a mummy of a woman, while the window on the fathers' side showed the lone derby hat of the Baron's.

Frank Thorne pressed his cane against the backs of Otis and Pyridine and pushed them towards the man.

"Now the moon, of pitiable repugnance falls on our eyes, what shall follow this wretched surprise." the young man said.

"We are here to find the Baron's son," Pyridine replied aloud while Otis secretly sulked.

"Who pray tell is asking?" said the young man.

"Goodbye Family Funeral."

"Ah, excellent. You're here already. I just received a message you were on your way. Little did I know it would be right after." The young man held his necklace as he examined them. Thereupon, he reached out to shake the Goodbyes hands: "I am Lord Zenwick, and this," directing to Frank Thorne, "is the Baron's son." Zenwick gestured to Thorne like a model showcasing a prize.

Frank Thorne was hardly what the Goodbyes imagined, and they wondered how Emma Blu could love such a man. "Why does he not have his father's name?"

"He took his mother's last name, Rose Thorne. She was quite a beauty in her time."

Zenwick looked longingly at Pyridine. "And what is your name, my lovely?" He said trying to kiss the back of her hand, but Otis moved in his hand in front to have it kissed instead. Zenwick stared at Otis blankly as he pulled his hand back. Otis recalled the name Zenwick and the bill from which he painfully had to deliver for him.

"This is my wife Pyridine," he blurted out, "and I believe I met your prophetic father through his little paper route delivering Zenwick bucks. My name is Otis." he said in a mocking tone.

"Your mistaken, I am the only Zenwick, but I do age creditably thanks to the well. I am sorry I don't recall you, but I do remember my bucks. They are a major currency in Nothom." The young man stood a moment in thought as Otis and Pyridine stood somewhat bewildered. "So yes, I have found my profit. Have you?"

"What order do you belong to?" Pyridine asked with a raised eyebrow.

"Disorder."

"Funny, we must be in the very same guild, and I don't recall you either?"

"You're delightful. It was meant to be a figure of speech, my dear. Even if I was in a guild, I am not aware of any guilds permitting women." He lifted his chin and continued to speak: "I abide by the stance that chaos of the elements needs harmony."

"Strange," replied Pyridine, "our guild has no restrictions, except perhaps for scared little men who might be afraid of a lady's touch, and our motto is quite the opposite; harmony lends itself to chaos."

"Touché," Zenwick said with a smile. "I am my own guild, and these are my disciples." He said referring to Thorne.

"Sorry," Otis piped in trying to move along their work, "Frank Thorne, I regret to inform you, your father has passed." Otis showed his finger with the rattails tied upon them.

Thorne looked blankly at Otis.

"Deceased. Kicked the bucket, went fishing, blew out his lamp, hung up his saddle, has sawdust in his beard, passed in his chips, he's shaking hands with St. Peter..."

"We get the point," yelled Zenwick. "And we know. I did call you to deliver his remains."

Otis shrugged. "Our mistake, he looked puzzled," Otis said referring to Thorne.

"Give them to me!" Zenwick said, pulling the circlet rattails off Otis' finger and directing to Thorne, "I think I have enough here to gather his essence."

"Sorry, we only put cents in the eyes when there is a body."

"His essence. His life's oil." Said Zenwick. "Oil is the energy of all life."

Pyridine raised a long fingernail in the air. "Funny, I thought labor is the energy of life, and I don't mean hard work."

"I am sure you have seen our elixir," Zenwick said raising his eyebrow to Otis. "I sent over free bottles to those poor miners when I heard the mine caved in. Those poor creatures need our spirits to lift them."

"Your tonic?"

"Yes, Chthonic. The "Ch" is silent. My tonic amplifies a distraction of the bacteria that is already in them. When a person is down, sometimes, they need a helping hand up."

"Making a person insane can be most distracting," replied Pyridine.

"You do have something there. The people I spoke to in Nicklesworth were oblivious," replied Otis.

"And why should they suffer anymore; haven't they been through enough? The Chthonic will rid their mind of sadness and fear so they can focus on work and making money."

Zenwick looked closer at Otis and took the hand of Pyridine. "Couldn't we all use a little more money? Debts and loans weigh us down. The Chthonic will take your mind off of it. The girl from tomorrow is here my lovely lady;" at that, he gave a sudden twirl and raised his arms to sing:

The girl from tomorrow,
Who claimed the benefits of the Yarrow.
Her placebo was unfound
Living richly downtown,
Hiding in her spaceship sombrero.

Disorder is better in the coven.
She said to a fourth cousin,
As she slept the day away
Making crochet.
Of dreams charred and sauteed in gourmet
Like warty frogs served in an oven.

"Louder, louder!" Everyday shouted.
Scaring the neighbors to hide.
Tantrum, gossip, and surprise,
Her actions would make them chide.

Petunias, peanuts, and buttons,
Until that time, she shut in.
Frightened, dismal, dismayed,
Of accidentally swallowing a bay.
Spending the rest of her time,
Quietly shut in.

He stopped short. "We are here to serve what people crave. Not what they need. We drain the oil of their life. It's what we do," he said proudly. "When someone drinks our Chthonic, it first numbs them of their worry, and then if they decide to consume more, it allows them for the proper guidance they need - to choose the harder decisions in life, so they don't have to."

"So you can control them," said Otis.

"To accept the drink is all their own. Besides, it gives my disciples purpose," Zenwick reassured. "You see they are all quite deranged until realizing they all have a PURPOSE. The corruption and destruction of one is the birth of another."

Thorne stood motionless.

Zenwick paced the room. "We can't just let anyone aboard this ship. No. We are looking for the right people to help me maneuver it. Without an active supply of followers, I will age, and then I won't be able to lead them. I need someone by my side if I am to take over the world. If you work for me, I can offer you anything you desire."

"He is a real dingbat," Otis said under his breath to his wife.

"Dingbats are not typical of these parts." returned Pyridine, before saying to Zenwick. "By chance may I have a sample myself?" She said opening her bag for a vial.

Zenwick smiled: "In time. Being is an exercise of care, my dear. Now for why you are really here."

Zenwick clapped his hands for attention. "Portals, we are speaking of. Portals. Opportunities. Look around you," he said, coaxing them towards the walled in caskets. "Don't be rude. Do say hello to them. They will have their smiles back in no time. That you can wager on and win."

"I can see you are in need of money."

"How do you know that?" inquired Otis.

"You are undertakers, are you not? In a world of zombies, an undertaker is obsolete."

Otis and Pyridine looked cold at one another.

"In salutation to our guests," Zenwick interrupted, "I will share another rhyme."

"Oh, please do not bore us with your hideous play on words," said Pyridine with his arms folded.

"But I am having all the fun, why not share it." said the sorcerer.

"Frankly, you're contagious," responded Otis.

Zenwick proceeded to dance around the room with the energy of youth. "Instead of hello, I will give you my regards. When saying Goodbye, I will likewise utter my respects." He twirled to the casket marked father and stopped, placing the rounded rattails on a hook under the derby hat. He removed the hat and flipped it on his head.

"And people think we are strange. He is more deranged than your Uncle Mute," Otis whispered to his wife.

"At least Mutey never told a bad joke."

"You know," Pyridine interrupted, backing up, "I just remembered we left the crematory stove on."

"Oh, I have one for you." Said Otis in thought. "What both contains a skeleton and also has something in common with a hearse and plans to rehearse?"

Zenwick thought for a moment. "Simple. A frame. For he knoweth our frame; he remembereth that we are dust."

"Nope, the answer is..." Otis took hold of Pyridine's hand, and raced to the door, when Zenwick called out: presenting the derby hat, pointing it at the couple and shouted: "Manifest!"

Frank Thorne looked at Otis and Pyridine with a devilish stare and tottered like a rabid wolf to stop them. Thorne, who was twice as strong from the lack of pain, dragged them back to his master.

Zenwick watched with glee as Zenwick did his bidding: "I can be motivated to take the chill out of children, the sill out of silly and any sense out of nonsense."

Pyridine stabbed at Thorne with her trocar, but he could feel nothing.

"Why would I?" Zenwick turned to Thorne, clapped and

commanded "Desist." Thorne stepped back from the two. Pyridine raised the pointy end of her trocar at Thorne and tried to cast a spell, "Above Cloudhome, Below Nothom, by the Great Mountain read my tome - send my attacker back to his home."

Strangely to Pyridine and Otis, the spell did nothing to change him but made a slight fizzle sound. "What, what? It doesn't normally do that?" she said in concern.

"You may try. But you will see your magic is not as strong as mine," replied Zenwick. "Thorne is under my direction now. He no longer feels. He has no heart."

The Goodbyes looked blankly in shock.

"I hate to say I told you so." Zenwick positioned himself next to Thorne and raised his arm in front of the Goodbyes. "Look at him carefully. Do you smell something rotting? You know, he was dead once. Your magic can only turn living things into your wishes, and Thorne, I'm afraid has been replaced by something, more, controllable."

"I take but a small tax of each for their everlasting life. It is not a lot, but a few years comes in handy to keep me looking and feeling young."

"You consume a piece of their souls?"

"I did not force anyone I assure you." he scolded. "They were all willing participants. In their state, they are absent of pain. Unaware of any corporeal changes. It's a fair trade in my book, considering I am alive, and they are dead."

"How about you write that into a haiku and mail it to us. In the meantime, we better be getting back to our clients. If you couldn't tell, we prefer dead things staying dead." Otis said forcefully.

"I intend to make the world a better place. A more harmonious place through the thoughts of one or if given a chance, the thoughts of another."

"Sounds rather dull."
"I will break your soul, of course."

"I take it you don't have children of your own?" Otis turned to say to Zenwick.

"I had a family once," said the sorcerer, "Never a child, but a dog nevertheless. My wife just loved to dress him up." his tone soured. "It was most appalling. If you do not make your passion your priority, you partake in trivialities like suits and hats for your dog."

To which the man shook his head, "You don't want to find yourself on the wrong side of our business." He argued.

"We currently are on the wrong side of the door." Pyridine insisted.

"Eventually you will find yourselves with nothing, and then nothing will become everything. See, EVERYTHING has nothing and only in something anything can ever be. Any more, and its just unearthing a pair of shelves. I beFore ever bE. Remember that illusion; it means the world!"

"Sounds absolutely pointless, but how do you factor a shelf out of nothing?" asked Otis.

Pyridine answered. "You subtract a caboodle and divide it by an oodle, leaving you with these two noodles."

"Okay, what if the question was "what is the whole enchilada of a lotta?" said Otis.

"I don't know, a side of chips?" replied Pyridine.

"That's brilliant P!" Said Otis, as he laughed nervously. However, Thorne and Zenwick were not laughing.

"All too clever!" The sorcerer said, calming his nerves. "You asked for a sample, now let us offer these Chthonic for yourselves."

Zenwick held his arms high in the air and chanted "socks, blocks, booka-choo-choo." Which magically made a glass of the tonic appear into Otis and Pyridine's hands.

"Completely on us," he said.

Pyridine nodded. "What a cute parlor trick."

"Considering you won't pay us," said Otis. "I think it may be due."

"I could double, no triple your salary if you would join us."

"Let me count that. Double zero is zero. Triple that is zero. Multiplied by zero is again zero. Divided by zero is ten. I think. You drive a hard bargain. But we don't want your charity. It seems like you are having a hard enough time getting your business off the ground."

Pyridine sniffed her drink, which had a similar pleasant aroma of her favorite dung beetle tea. Otis who had a nose for smelling thought it smelled more like burning horse's hooves when being shod. The scent was enticing, but he had more common sense and brought it away from Pyridine's lips.

Zenwick commanded Thorne and forced the drink to the weary

lips of Otis. Pyridine was unable to stop him, but instead shouted: "Enough!"

Zenwick halted Thorne to listen.

"Otis," Pyridine, said with a pause. "Put on your big boy pants and do as the man says."

"But it's poison."

"Must you always complain," she quibbled, seeing Zenwick's renewed attention, and realizing it was in her best interest to chastise her husband. "To think against all the omens and curses upon me I still married you. Obviously, I made that mistake initially, but I won't make it again."

Otis sniffled with tears in his eyes. "What are you saying?" Taking the cup from Thorne and feebly sipping. "Look, I'm drinking it."

"I've had it with you. Our trip is a disaster. We can't afford it, and then you expect me to rekindle our flame?"

"I knew I failed you." He said bawling.

Zenwick clapped and cheered, "Leave him," reaching out his hand to take hers. "He is feeble and worthless. You are a witch of higher standards. No human can meet your match."

"I have made up my mind," Pyridine said removing out of her brassiere the Chromus Humbug broach.

"You found the Chromus Humbug!" Otis said in shock. "That was for our rekindling. Where did you find it?"

"Otis, you are always losing things. I've decided now it's time to be on the winning team."

"No, Pyridine, you don't know what you're saying. Don't give it to him. You will break our bond." He begged.

"We are in terrible money crisis, and a witch must be able to afford to conjure."

"You must be under his spell," Otis cried.

"No," she argued, "I have come to my senses."

"What about the family?" Otis reasoned. Meanwhile, his stove top hat too was in a panic and quickly embraced the trocar. "I will change, I can work extra at the Blacksmith shop."

"Quiet Otis. I've shared my mind and will not change it. We've spent many moons together, struggling under your bad leadership. You've had your chance."

This stirred the fervent emotion of the sorcerer to see Otis balled like a child, that he chuckled. "If you are certain Pyridine, take my hand and leave this mortal."

"Very good," Zenwick congratulated, "you are making the right choice with you by my side, we will rule the world."

She took the symbol of their rekindling and threw it at the feet of Zenwick. "I agree to work for you on one condition."

Pyridine stepped forward to the sorcerer and took his hand. Pyridine looked dreamily into his eyes. "Surely, what is it?" He asked.

"I must have you."

Chapter XXII. Pyridine's Remorse

Pyridine stood before Zenwick and fluttered her lashes to his amazement and momentarily entrancing him.

"Let this broach be our engagement." Pyridine said, holding it up to Zenwick's eyes.

"What an exquisite piece of jewelry," Zenwick examined it and said briefly, removing the Baron's hat and placing it by his side. "But not as exquisite as you." he directed, taking her hand.

"This is terrible. I'm nothing." wept Otis in the corner and no longer fighting Thorne's grip.

Pyridine could sense the sorcerer was opening his heart. "I must have you," she continued.

Pyridine held the Chromus Humbug tightly in her palm and held her hand up for his kiss. He obliged and just as he did Pyridine pierced the bug's stomach with her sharp fingernail. "I must have you dead," she cried, crushing it. The toxins within wafted upwards into Zenwick's gaping mouth. Momentarily mesmerized by the green strains of smoke, she quickly backed away and covered her nose with her dress. Zenwick was shocked but vulnerable. The sorcerer tried in vain to place the derby hat back onto his head and conjure a last-second shield of his own. But in a moment he fell to his knees choking from the odor. Pyridine covered Otis's face as they watched Zenwick feel the toxins surge through his body. "Thorne, do something." he coughed and rattled on the floor, clasping his throat. Thorne broke through the foul vapors and limped to his master's aid, but little could be done. Zenwick began aging rapidly, returning all the years that he had stolen. His hair grew white and fell out in chunks, and his skin wrinkled tightly over his bones. His eyes flashed open and shut in pain, seeing the luster of youth exit his pupils.

The Goodbyes took back the valuable rattails, placing it into Otis' pocket, and hurried out of the room.

Chapter XXIII. Feeling Scrappy

Once outside, Pyridine gently coaxed her husband back to reality as he questioned her, "But I thought you wanted him, not me?"

"That was just a scheme to trick him. There was no way I was drinking that vile stuff."

"So, you didn't mean all those things you said?"

"You do complain a lot," she laughed.

"And what about our vow? The Chromis Humbug?"

"I do regret that. But Otis, you should have known it was all a lie. I've never been under your leadership, you know a witch is always in charge." She said with a gentle brush against his cheek to his smile. "Besides with what you drank, you won't remember any of this in the morning. I assure you." Pyridine frowned slightly, knowing she had to give up the beautiful broach to keep them safe.

Suddenly they heard a loud commotion from one of the oil drills. "I hope they did not upset Orphie!"

It was a free-for-all boxing match and shootout as Pyridine

ducked behind the giant *potatoe* sculpture to see, pulling Otis with her.

"What is it?" asked Otis. "What do you see?"

Orphie was restless and had about enough of this so-called vacation and was tossing the guards right and left like rag dolls, kicking some, hurling others, bullets were going off, it was a most frantic tantrum. She used one of the zombie guard's they referred to as "Banjo" to whip around like a bat.

"I am sick of this vacation." Orphie screamed, batting Banjo at a zombie in hiding, "I am tired of this food. I can't stand these people. And quit calling me a monster!" Thankfully Orphie, who was quite short, was not hurt like the guards. But according to Zenwick, they were dead already, so it didn't quite matter if they had a few extra bruises. Several stray bullets poked holes in the side of the sculpture.

"This potato is all poked and ready for baking," Otis said peeking around the sculpture. He then proceeded to call the action like a prize fight, unconcerned with his daughter's safety. After all, this was no ordinary child, with the strength of her great grandfather King Konzo, a circus strongman that mated with a monstrous sea banshee named Queen Bacillus.

"Orphie comes out and throws two jabs and a left hook. Banjo walks forward but walks right into two body shots. The first KO of the night. A string of rights, and lefts, Orphie continues to press forward and is now swinging Banjo at the outlaws. Orphie lands a handful of direct blows to the bodies. One in the black hat fires off two shots to both sides of Banjo. A second outlaw strikes his rifle at Orphie but really takes it to Banjo with an uppercut. This is not Banjo's night. Now Orphie is being blasted from both sides with gunfire but all into Banjo again. Orphie comes right back with three swings of Banjo to their heads and bodies. The last man is stepping back and misses his shot though Orphie lands another hard flying left hook to his head, knocking him out into the hanging supper bell."

DING DING DING!

"That's the bell, another glorious victory for the champ!"

Pyridine collected her family. "Please contact us again if you should need any mortuary arrangements." She then turned to her daughter and scolded: "When we get home there will be no Borealis pudding for you child. Such a mess you've made."

"Yes, indeed." returned the father, "but what a showing!"

Dorian crawled out of Orphie's pocket and helped wrap the zombies in its webbing to prevent them from following the family, but it was not enough for Frank Thorne appeared from the mission, lurching after the Goodbyes.

Chapter XXIV. A Nose for Rain

The Goodbyes with Dorian in Orphie's pocket ran as far as they could, pausing underneath an oil rig. They could see Thorne in the distance getting closer. At the same time, the three sat hiding under the lofty rig, and the elixir was starting to soak into Otis's veins. "Can you smell that?" Otis said with fever.

"My nose tells me the rain is close."

"Hold his tongue, " called out Pyridine to her daughter. "Otherwise, Thorne will hear us."

Unfortunately, Otis wouldn't stand still, and in wild chimpanzee-like behavior, he flung his arms, slapped the ground and stomped, making Orphie laugh and giving up their location quickly to Thorne.

Soon, Orphie forgot why they were hiding and instead insisted: "Let's go play!" to which she grabbed Otis and ran into the middle of the oil field.

"Otis! Orphie!" Pyridine screamed trying to grab them. "You'll get yourself killed!"

Thorne stopped and watched readying a position behind a boulder as Otis and Orphie were giggling and chasing one another.

Orphie was the first to see Thorne's hideout. "Look dad," she exclaimed, "It's that prickle guy!"

"Where!" cried Otis trying to skip to his daughter. "Where's the pickle guy?" Orphie laughed and pointed to the outlaw whom Otis confirmed it was, in fact, him because of the bullet that wooshed past their heads.

WOOSH!

"Let's go see if he's dill or sweet?" Otis said drunkenly, and absent of discernment. "I bet he's a dill."

Thorne raised his revolver again to the easy target. Pyridine stayed under the oil rig and desperately tried to think of a spell to protect them, circling her trocar above her head she cast: "Great Mountain, Great Mountain, north, south, east and west. I ask for your protection. Negative energy lift. Make my Otis and Orphie agile and swift."

It was then, the rain began to trickle down, and lightning flashed in the sky. Otis raced after Thorne with Orphie on his heels as Dorian hung by a string still attached to Orphie's head. Thankfully Thorne's second shot jammed and had to be cleared. In this matter of seconds, Thorne's targets disappeared from sight.

"Yoohoo. Where did ya go?" Thorne said peeking out.

When suddenly Otis chirped from the other end of the boulder. "Dreary day!" before ducking again behind the rock.

Thorne fired off his gun at the spot.

WIZZ!

But it was late, "Try that again!" he cried.

Otis was followed by Orphie who had met her father and decided to partake in the greeting. She popped out from another corner of the boulder behind Thorne and said: "Dreary day!" jumping back to their amusement. Thorne fired a second shot but also missed.

POP!

Thorne grunted in torment, as he picked himself up with the cane to investigate the other side of the boulder.

The outlaw hobbled around the rock to shoot the first head he would see from the fungus covered boulder, but as none came, he believed they might have gotten behind him. He spun and fired another round.

BAM!

But Otis and Orphie snuck at the same moment quietly on the other side of the rock and again popped out at two new sides of the boulder while Pyridine looked disapprovingly swirling the magic trocar testing another spell that might thwart off the attack:

"Great Mountain, Great Mountain, north, south, east and west. I ask for your assistance. Break the fence. Make the struggle come to their sense."

Otis crouched down behind the rock with his daughter. Orphie was full of mischief but could not figure out why her father seemed to be enjoying himself so much. After a short time, Thorne peaked around the massive stone, but this time could not see anyone but Pyridine under the oil rig. While his head was turned Otis and Orphie sprung up in front of the boulder and said with a start, "Are you looking for someone?" knocking Thorne backward, and discharging his firearm once more, ricocheting off the rock.

PEW!

The lightning lit up the sky overhead as Thorne swung his cane at the two, but Orphie took hold of the other end as the two yanked it back and forth while she said: "Tug of war. Tug of war." Until Orphie, with her unnatured strength, spun the cane so hard she picked him several feet off the ground and tumbled him into the wet dirt. Unharmed, Dorian also flew out of her pocket, and tried to get in on the action.

"You lost, and I won." she cried happily.

The crooked man picked himself up. "Your dead meat!" He cried, wiping the dirt from his eyes. He tried to reload his revolver when Otis sunk against him in drunken affection, "I just wanted to say," he slurred, "how this a real treat for us to find a man of your delinquency in the middle of a rainstorm." At the same moment, Orphie playfully jumped on Thorne's back to the boom of thunder, "Give me a piggyback ride. Wheee!" The gun was kicked from Thorne's hand, and his off-balance body fell as Otis and Orphie wrestled him in the mud. Pyridine coached from the sidelines screaming, "Give him the King Konzo death hold!"

Thorne could not reach his knife and struggled to make an escape from the two, punching and kicking, but Orphie and Otis only giggled. "Quit, that tickles!" And they tickled him right back.

"SHUT IT, SHUT IT!" Howled Thorne. "Get off me and shut your traps!"

Otis and Orphie paused to look curiously at each other. "Did we leave some open?" before wrestling again.

"That's it!" Thorne reached to his hip for his knife but saw it had fallen behind the Goodbyes. The cane, however, was near his feet and he lifted it like a lance between them.

"Stand aside or lose your heads!" Thorne threatened.

"He is good at this game!" Otis replied.

Behind the boulder, Pyridine was juggling the spider in one hand and the trocar in the other.

"Let's play a different game, like hunt the slipper." said Orphie, who then chanted "Undertaker, undertaker, mend the departed, look at Thorne he smells like he farted."
"No, no."

"Pin the tail on the outlaw?" Otis said as a boom of thunder and lightning followed his proposal.

"All right." Thorne whipped the cane around. "How about we play hide and seek?"

"My daughter is a master of hide and shriek, you'll never win."

"I'll take my chance." said the outlaw huffing.

The storm grew heavier and the lightning lit up the sky. Pyridine snuck behind them and saw her way to Thorne's gun. As the outlaw approached with a hobble, she ducked behind the boulder. Orphie and Otis said to Thorne: "Have at it. We don't mind the rain. In fact, the smelly feet odor of this boulder is atrocious, making it the perfect place for us to sit and count." The two went on discussing the rules to hear, "After he goes, I want to be it, and you have to find me," said Otis to his daughter drenched in the rain.

Thorne limped in front of Otis and Orphie who sat crisscrossed with their eyes closed and prepared to swing his crooked rifle at Otis. "Playtime is over," he called out.

Chapter XXV. The Disturbed

Frank Thorne was about to bat Otis with his bent rifle when he suddenly found himself outflanked by Pyridine at his side with his own gun. "Put the rifle down you decaying necrotic tissue," she ordered.

Thorne turned to her as she held the trocar in one hand and the revolver in the other.

"Go ahead and shoot. Everyone else has. I might just feel something." The outlaw reached out and pulled the firearm towards him blowing a small hole into his already cratered chest.

POW!

"Aww mom," said Orphie, looking up at the two, "why did you have to go and ruin our game?"

"He meant to kill you."

It was then, Thorne saw a twinkling in Pyridine's eyelashes that drew him to her eyes. There in the iris, he saw something move, Thorne used the crook of his cane to pull her in closer to see. It was not of his own reflection but a stranger in his place.

"Let go of me," she said digging her sharp nails in his numb arms.

He stood gazing, studying her eyes that shone like mirrors. Perhaps it was the spell Pyridine cast or Thorne's reoccurring visions, but he could now see himself with his beloved holding her hand reminding him of a better time. In a split second the vision faded, and his perspective changed looking down at him self: seperated. He was lying on a gurney with Zenwick standing over. Zenwick wore his father's derby hat upon his head and Thorne's body was attached to several mechanical instruments poking him with needles. He was still alive but very much asleep from the tonic and as he felt the jabs from the scientist he came to and his perspective or conscious nearly rejoined with his body as he tried to open his eyes and live again. But Zenwick placed his cruel hands over Thorne's neck and strangled him, taking away the last gasp of air and any chance of freedom. What happened next was most evil indeed for the essence inside the bottle, of a terrible soul from the underworld, took control. Thorne's dead eyes fluttered as Zenwick spoke: "My subject. Welcome to your new life. Awake. Manifest." Thorne's cadaver sat up unable to protest and lifted its head to face his master. Saliva dripped from his mouth and his dry eyes opened and began to turn a different color from amber to a hazel gray. This announced the arrival of the new host and was the final step in reviving the dead.

Zenwick's voice continued as he heard his name "Thorne. Thorne. Thorne," until at once Zenwick, in full body, was behind him, breaking the spell and erasing the vision. "Good work Thorne, I see you have caught all of our fleeting birds." Zenwick was now old, gray and weak, again wearing the hat of the Baron. He was haggard from the Chromus Humbug's poison that would have killed any other man had he not stolen so many lives himself. "Let's get rid of these little monsters once and for all."

Orphie stomped in the dust. "The only monster I've seen on this trip is you," she said angrily.

Thorne felt his heart murmur, struggling with the vision of Zenwick.

"What are you waiting for?" Zenwick insisted.

Thorne paused.

"Did you hear me Thorne? Put them out of their misery."

"We don't mind the misery as long as it's nicely wrapped," said Otis.

Zenwick took hold of hat. "Kill them!" Zenwick yelled. "Manifest!"

Thorne robotically snatched his revolver and swiftly fired at the three! CLICK. CLICK. CLICK. CLICK. CLICK. CLICK. The gun chamber rolled over twice causing the Goodbye's to think they had already been shot, when in reality Thorne fired none.

"I think we all could use that extra pair of pants now," mumbled Orphie.

"Reload, you fool," coughed Zenwick.

Thorne obeyed and started to reload but was again enchanted by the haunting specter of the Baron in his mind. *"Look at what Zenwick has made of you."* A disembodied voice said to him, *"Do not listen to him, I am your true master."* Thorne crouched back swatting the voice like a fly. "No! Get outta' my head!"

"What are you babbling about?" cried Zenwick.

Thorne dropped the revolver into the dirt and left hobbling away and swatting the air in delusions.

They all watched in shock before turning their attention to the revolver that sat in the dirt! In a mad scramble, the Goodbye's and Zenwick dove for the gun.

BANG!

The revolver discharged and fired at the diving head of Otis. His tall top hat flew off his head, and immediately, the magic trocar, that so loved the magic hat, ripped from Pyridine's hand and took flight, rocketing towards Zenwick. The trocar speared through his chest with such grave force that the tip pierced out the other side and lifted him high into the air taking him off to be destroyed into the clouds of thunder and lightning.

Pyridine and Orphie quickly attended Otis with Dorian's healing webbing in tow and could see there was no wound in his head, except for black residue from the gun. They sat Otis up, who had the mind to say: "My poor crown." To which the family knew he was not physically harmed but more mentally aware, and that only his beloved hat had suffered the bullet wound.

Orphie's parents grew a slight tear in their eyes. "I've lost a perfectly good trocar," Pyridine said looking to the flashing heavens above, "however temperamental she was."

The three looked back in awe above them seeing Zenwick bounce around from one cloud to the other being struck several times by lightning as his dust fell over them.

Pyridine thought wisely to take a few scraps of his dust that sprinkled down to use perhaps later in an antidote potion. "Never know when you might need a speck of the disturbed, it can really wake up a party!"

Otis mournfully picked up his top hat that had been hollowed out from the gun blast.

"We should bury what is left of your hat." Orphie said

mournfully.

"It was a good hat."

"It was a good trocar."

Otis who had a small pocket spade handy, presented it to Orphie for she did most all of the digging. With all her might Orphie struck the spade down into the ground removing dirt and jabbed with one final heavy thrust something underneath that quickly spewed a geyser to appear.

"It's that oil again!" said Pyridine. "Must be from a pipe."

Otis joined Orphie dancing in the oil.

At the same time, and unknown to them, in an hour the engine room of the mission had completely overheated from the oil pipe that Orphie broke into, and stopped operating altogether.

By the time they were finished, the rain had subsided, and the Goodbyes began to worry again, for they would not be in Nothom on time. They leaned against the fungus covered boulder where the plants had a foul foot stench.

Otis began sniffing his surroundings catching the smell. "Hey I know that," he comforted. "I believe a shortcut is nearby." He brushed away the years of leaves and found a keyhole within the rock. "I found it! I found it!" He said joyfully. "The rock is Nothom's belly button."

"His belly button, father?"

"You sure you are not just feeling the effects of the tonic?"

"Yes, he must have been an outie! It has all the characteristics of one." Otis illuminated to Orphie and Pyridine, directing them to the yellowish overhang and the fungus that grew on it.

"What would we do without that nose of yours?" They laughed together.

Otis snickered but struggled to take the Nothom key from his coat as the tonic was slowing his movement. With the assistance of his wife, she found the key sloshing in pickle juice and placed it in the lock turning it to the right. The toenail slid open, and the Goodbyes walked in carefully into total darkness.

In a moment they were inside a slide-like tunnel which brought them back down to Nothom where they could see again their carriage and horse, Midnight chewing on a branch of a frizzled hair tree, while the Posy Palace gleamed across from it.

Chapter XXVI. Posy Palace

Pyridine volunteered to check them in as Otis was quickly becoming lethargic to speak properly, another side effect of the Chthonic. "We will be staying for a moon's phase," she said to a bellman. Orphie piled on several mortician's bags into the bellman's hands that they retrieved from their carriage. "Be careful, try not to shake the methanol unless you want to turn blue."

Orphie took her father over her shoulder while she presented a tip of a small pewter box into the servant's breast pocket. The bellman peered down as several bugs slithered out.

"What is that?" he said in fright.

"Leeches mostly. Do you have a headache?"

"I do now," he said aloud.

"Than you are most welcome."

The bellhop led the family to the front desk, and Pyridine tapped the desk bell several times to the sound of Chopin's funeral march: Dum dum da dum—dum da dum—da dum da dum.

The entry was brandished in dark wood and pillars held a second-floor balcony with posy themed carpeting and fixtures lighting up the room.

"Enjoy your stay." The bellhop tossed the casket and bags at their feet before escaping.

"Rather a strange fellow. Did you give him the tip I told you?" asked Pyridine to her daughter.

"Yes, mother."

"Great, nothing more valuable than the Baron's foot long leeches. A remedy that will always toe the mark."

"When do you get to see Grandma?" asked the child.

"After we check in, let's see if she can help carry her son."

Orphie propped Otis against the front desk.

"May I help you?" asked the receptionist.

"Yes, checking in under Goodbye," said Pyridine.

"Yes, you must be Goliath Goodbye?"

"No, although people sometimes confuse me."

"Grimm and Glumm Drop Goodbye?"

"No last I checked I had only one head."

"Fecal Goodbye?"

"Nada. He lives down under."

"Chicken Liver, Kepla, Fibroid, Canker Sore?"

"No - though I'm beginning to fear for our family medical history."

"Madam. We have over a hundred Goodbyes registered. What is your name?"

"Pyridine Goodbye, of course."

"Right." He said frazzled and rapidly turning the pages. The man was about to give up when he came to the final page and the very last line. "Otis and Pyridine Goodbye."

"That's the one or two," Otis slurred out.

"Fine! Room 3327," he said in defeat, dropping the key into Pyridine's hands. "A luxury suite to die for."

"I should certainly hope so," said she.

The front desk agent gave the Goodbyes a gift basket which included jars of Purple Leaf Selects, the Hungry Villager, and Villager Choice, which were bound together with a bow.

"Lovely, we have something to feed the rats."

They ascended three flights of stairs, with Orphie carrying most of the bags, and turned right into room 3327.

The first two floors were of the original puddled black rugs and dungeon gray wallpaper. While the third floor had been remodeled in pink and teal posies.

Unfortunately to the Goodbyes, the room was hideous and they thought for a moment they had reached the chamber in error. The brightly colored walls had been dusted and swept of all creepy things, including rats. The furniture was whitewashed, and the view was not the Lake of Fire, but a hot spring called the Pit of Despair, and sadly it was not a worthy view when someone was wading in it was named Hope, whom they were promptly greeted by.

"Hi, I'm Hope, come in, the water is refreshing," she yelled up to them, staring out the window.

Upon seeing the pit outside their window, further disappointment fell on the faces of our dear Goodbye Family. Lounging guests surrounded the spring while a phonograph spouted happy songs about love.

"A Pool of Merriment!? Looks more like a pond of depressing," said Orphie wisely.

They at once marched back down to the desk and clicked the bell again to Chopin's Funeral March: Dum dum da dum—dum da dum—da dum da dum.

The front desk agent's manager tried to calm them, "Can I interest you in a free cruise on the Sea of Rejoice?"

"Is there any moaning and wailing?"

"I'll book you for the morning cruise, and you are guaranteed to see whales then."

"No!" declared Pyridine, "the Pool of Merriment, really what were you thinking?"

The manager leaned forward and whispered. "Don't you just love it? We filled it in with the finest sandstone and turned the old lake into a hot spring. We are trying to shake the negative connotation the old name carried with it, while still keeping the edginess that attracts people. So we call it the Pool of Merriment instead. The tourists love it, and they don't even have to get burned to a cinder."

"I don't like it. This hotel is terribly run."

The front desk manager ignored her comment. "Can I interest you in free tickets to a sporting event instead?"

"Does it include you running around a ring with a hungry lion?" asked Pyridine angrily.

The agent looked bewildered. "You are absurd!"

Orphie then pointed out a very narrow door attached to the lobby and pulled their luggage and her parents toward it. They might have stayed disagreeing with the front desk agent if Orphie had not seen it. In fact, it was mistakenly the broom closet she brought them to. The manager who was exhausted by it all agreed, "Fine, take the broom closet, whatever you want. Just leave me alone."

The closet measured 2 feet wide by 7 feet long. It had no light, a musty sewer smell, and most of the space was already occupied by brooms and tools.

Otis propped his arms over his head in comfort. "It just goes to prove if you don't complain you might not get an upgrade like this."

Chapter XXVII. The Big Chill

They went about making themselves at home - however, what they didn't realize is that Otis's mother Yeast and her cat Ouiji had already claimed it for themselves. Orphie was the first to spy the old woman's gray tangles of hair that were indistinguishable from the mops.

"Grandma!" said Orphie jumping with excitement.

A black cat with an oversized head popped out of Yeast's suitcase and began to nuzzle Orphie's legs. "That one's name is Ouiji," she said instructing as Orphie pet him. "He seems to like you." "You may have HER." She said to the cat rather than the child to the cat.

"May I?" Orphie turned to her mother.

"Your father is likely allergic, but he is allergic to most things. If you care for him, I don't see why not."

Ouiji sniffed around Otis's jacket. "Are you hungry fellow?" Orphie said searching through her father's pockets to find something for it to eat. There were keys, tools, the circlet rattails, and pickles - and the cat eagerly ate a pickle and whatever else it could fit into its ravenous mouth. Orphie continued to look in her father's pockets and found the shiny star that belonged to the sheriff of Nicklesworth and decided to wear it on her dress.

"Do I look fancy grandma?"

"Yes indeed. A pentagram is always a nice touch."

At this moment, Ouiji coughed up a hairball that landed in the lap of Orphie.

"Don't mind that, he does that from time to time," Yeast advised. "Unusual shape, that one."

On closer examination the hairball was the crusty and thready circlet rattails the cat had unknowingly regurgitated. Orphie thought it looked creepy and interesting and decided to put it back into Otis's pocket for safekeeping.

After freshening up, the Goodbyes proceeded to the back of a long line cued in the hallway leading to the courtyard where everyone would meet. Orphie was having difficulty standing in line, and her tantrum escalated from pressing her head firmly into her mother's stomach to sliding to the floor and flopping over. Thankfully Orphie did not weigh as much as her strength, ten men or an elephant, and after a moment was picked up and slunk onto her mother's shoulders.

They entered the dimly lit courtyard and realized it was hard to recognize those beside them, with immediate families in clusters, the Goodbyes could see their Cousins Grimm and Glumm, but these two couldn't stop chatting between their two heads. Several familiar voices were heard through the air including Yeast's cackling which was the loudest of all. Pyridine gave their name as Goodbye-Leech as Leech was her maiden name and thus would seat their families closer together. The host announced their names and Pyridine carried Orphie on her shoulders, Orphie carried Ouiji, Ouiji carried Dorian, while Yeast carried Otis.

The courtyard was now torchlit, and they could see around them the ornamentals intermixed with garden hemlock, skunk cabbage, which grew naturally and planted posies surrounding the dreaded wellness pool at its center which now was vacant of visitors and served as staging for a band.

The host then introduced the courtyard's several buffet areas. There were the usual entries: Baked Gall of Goat, Eye Creme of Newt Soup, Whipped Basilik drizzled in Snake Oil Sauce, to name a few. While also more exotic dishes perked up the guests including Potatoes Au Kraken and Fairy Cacciatore.

They surveyed the entrees and took their seats, where they were asked what they would like to drink: Drowned Finch Tea or Ice Hemlock.

Their specific server was named Boris, but a handful took part in the serving including an Igor. At the table across from them sat the

Boil family who was related through the Leech's.

To Pyridine's left sat Fibroid, who was patiently waiting for his wife Yeast (who you now know was Otis's parents). Sir Spekulum sat alone at a child's table with his shield and armor, no one was quite sure as to why. Pyridine's parents, Goiter and Yannick the Wicked, sat quietly to her right (they didn't talk much).

The sound of broken glass was occasionally heard under the choir of cheers and laughs as they delved into their favorite dishes. Orphie placed a cyclops eye to her own for a chuckle and Otis feeling faint responded with falling face first into a bucket full of ice. They all felt fully stuffed, except that is Otis who rested peacefully in the ice bucket. Pyridine checked his pulse and since he still was resting, she believed he was at least preserved with the ice if he should expire while she caught up with the family.

At the end of dinner, Pyridine feared her husband might need an emergency revival. She took from her purse the vial of Disturbed she collected from Zenwick's dust and lifted Otis's head out of the ice. She was about to sprinkle the vial into his ear, but his ear was so plugged with ear wax, having not made candles from it in months, that she was forced to try and get it into his nostril. This also failed due to the tangled nose hairs that brutishly fought off the vial.

So Orphie spread his right nostril open and tipped his head back as Pyridine clipped his tangling nose hairs that seemed to pop out like a forest of spider legs. However, the procedure was much too difficult to simply apply and hope it would not get absorbed by his dense nostril hair. As she cut, the hair grew back, and so Pyridine asked Orphie to retrieve her tarantula. They again all set into place with the child holding his nose, but this time while Pyridine cut a path of his nose hairs, Dorian assisted with the small bottle into its front legs and snuck itself inside his nose and dropped the contents into his nasal passage.

It was a delicate task, and after a moment, Otis was about to sneeze scaring everyone into thinking he might project the medicine and the tarantula with it. But thinking quickly, Pyridine combed her husband's mustache with his Pterodactyl comb and soothed the urge. Orphie carefully carried Dorian back out, and it only took a minute for Otis to revive. However now more intensely excited than his regular silly self. He placed the cold ice bucket back over his head, and banged himself about, then slowed to a turtle's pace, and instantly back again. It took a few minutes for the medicine to fully kick in, as he went back and forth from warp speed to a crawl, but once it did he could not stop moving his feet, and sweating which Pyridine knew was a known side effect.

"I feel much better, yes, I do!"

Pyridine asked her daughter, "Orphie my little bat, have you learned your lessons today?"

"To not act like father?"

"Sure, that's good enough, I think."

At this time, the dancing began and Otis, who was sweating profusely, swelled in the bucket. The room laughed with him, and he continued sharing his praise for the party guests around the room. "Dreary Day!" he said most jovially. Pyridine kept her distance mingling, seeing her husband silly but at least lively self again.

The band took the stage consisting of five cowboy dudded skeletons that used their stretchy veins to string around their instruments. The band was called The Hip Bones and was fronted by a banjo player who sang and a backup team of an accordion, guitar, violin, and upright bass.

The Hip Bones started with a bang and the song went something like this:

Who tied that crape on the door?
Oh, who tied that crape on the door?
It's ugly, it's smugly,
it's downright fugly.
Look up, dear, for what's in store.
Death tied that crape on the door.

The melody repeated like this until Otis after having drunk the Chthonic and had been sprinkled with the Disturbed was so bizarre with his dancing, flailing and hopping around like a frog, the song came to a close and he was the only one still standing with the ice bucket firmly stuck over his head.

The crowd was silent watching Otis intently as he lowered to one knee.

"P," he announced, "I know I don't have a (hiccup)...Chromus Humbug anymore, nor riches that you deserve..." he said rather tinny and facing away from her. Orphie quickly guided her father back to her mother's direction. "But would you (hiccup) consider rekindling our flame?"

Pyridine lifted Otis off the floor with the bucket still on his head. "Yes of course," she said, "my little buboes." To the delight of the crowd.

Otis searched through his pockets forgetting he no longer had the Chromus Humbug. "Wait, my bat, I nearly forgot I have to retie the knot." At this, he felt a ring inside his pocket and knowing very little about it and presented it to the hand of Pyridine.

"How dreadful." Pyridine said with a smile, admiring the hairy and crusty circlet rattails that had been digested and regurgitated from the cat's stomach.

Orphie and the rest of the clan clapped and cheered, rattling the ground so much with their hard dancing that a small crack opened the hot springs with a bright bubbly fire that burst out and

illuminated the darkness above. Soon it boiled over, filling the courtyard, and forcing the patrons out the exits. It was the Lake of Fire reclaiming its grounds and the black sky overhead smoked red hot dimming the oil tubes or what some thought were stars. Above they could now see the firey eruption over a grey stream of current air, a twinkling of the past renewed.

The tables set with their dinners shook and the ground trembled. "Earthquake!" One of the family members yelled, causing the rest to panic. Pyridine watched in excitement admiring her ring and sipping her Ice Hemlock. Yeast was too busy corraling her terrified cats that jumped from person to person knocking off wigs and hats. Orphie sat with her mother calmly brushing her cat Ouiji, but the shaking did jostle Dorian the spider afixed again to her hair. Otis had fallen upside down looking ever so much like a plant with his head stuck in the bucket and arms and legs up in the air.

What came next though was spectacular for the Goodbyes and the world of Nothom. The dance floor completely cracked open and shown through the Lake of Fire it had been built upon. In a second, the bubbling magma overtook the stage as things began to slowly fall in. It was quite serious and the party had to exit quickly while Pyridine still had a look of fascination. It was after all the Goodbyes joyous renewal and physical manifestation of it in Nothom.

By the end of the night, Otis's greasy hair and sweat eventually lifted the bucket off his head and after a healthy dose of snacking on pickles his nerves settled.

Pyridine wisely came to realize that the tonic was not fool proof. As it turned out, and by examining Otis, Pyridine deduced that by eating a pickle, or more precisely anything pickled as was in the case of Hibiscus, that the correct antidote was a pickle's acidic solution, and could flush the bloodstream of the tonic.

"You know Otis, I believe fermentation is the answer."

Chapter XXVIII. In a Pickle

The following morning, the Goodbyes arrived back home to find Emma, Hibiscus and Professor Lint cowering in the corner of their parlor with Mrs. Everyday blocking their path. She was quite stiff and terrifying and seemed to be awaiting a command.

"Can you give us some help?" Piped up Emma. "She's been staring at us for the last twelve hours."

"And I gotsa pee!" said the Professor.

"And I already did." replied Hibiscus.

So the Goodbye's crept up behind Mrs. Everyday and Otis took a pickle from his pocket and crammed it into her mouth. She was forced to chew it and after it's taste she fell to the floor with a twitch and belch releasing the venomous soul. "There goes the essence." Everyone in the room pinched their nose for the smell was that of a spoiled bratwurst. Orphie crawled over to check Mrs. Everyday. "Dead as a doornail," she happily reported.

"That's a relief," said Pyridine. "Now let's get this house aired out, the insects inside, and get back to business!"

"I'm with you P," seconded Otis.

"Me too," answered Orphie.

"Mrooww, " said their new cat Ouiji.

"Eep," finished the Pinpoint Tarantula.

Having seen the antidote at work, Emma, the Professor and Hibiscus also went back to town and offered up their last jars of Purple Leaf Selects to give to the comatose.

Nicklesworth in time would revive, and with the blacksmith counted as one of the dead and a high need for the undertaker in town, Otis moved his extra carriages and woodworking tools into the blacksmith shop while they kept their tree home seperate for the wakes and funerals. Orphie too, thought of how she might keep things better in order by appointing her self as sheriff. Once again the business was booming to the delight of Pyridine, who was able to afford a new trocar, and Otis a top hat. In very little time, Orphie playfully bewitched the hat and trocar again, stirring a new romance in the Goodbye household while an old romance was rekindled thanks to the crusty rattails happily worn on Pyridine's finger.

THE END

OTHER TITLES BY LORIN MORGAN-RICHARDS

Simon Snootle and Other Small Stories (2009)

A Boy Born from Mold and Other Delectable Morsels (2010)

A Little Hard to Swallow (2010)

A Welsh Alphabet (2010), with notes by Peter Anthony Freeman

The Terribly Mini Monster Book (2011)

Me 'ma and the Great Mountain (2012), with foreword by Corine Fairbanks

Welsh in the Old West (2015), with foreword by Jude Johnson

Dark Letter Days: Collected Works (2016)

The Night Speaks to Me: A Posthumous Account of Jim Morrison (2016)

The People of Turtle Island: Book One in the Series (2016)

The Dreaded Summons and Other Misplaced Bills (2017)

Imperfectualism (2020)

OTHER TITLES BY LORIN MORGAN-RICHARDS
(continued)

The Goodbye Family and the Great Mountain (2020)

Comic collections by Lorin Morgan-Richards, as of 2020

Memento Mori: The Goodbye Family Album (2017)

Wanted: Dead or Alive...but not stinkin' (2017)

The Goodbye Family Unveiled (2017)

Down West (2018)

Nicklesworth: Featuring the Goodbye Family (2018)

Gallows Humor: Hangin' with the Goodbye Family (2018)

Dead Man's Hand-kerchief: Dealing with the Goodbye Family (2019)

The Importance of Being Otis: Undertaking with the Goodbye Family (2019)

Yippee Ki-Yayenne Mother Pepper: Getting Saucy with the Goodbye Family (2019)

Pyridine's Fancy: It's a Grave Business with the Goodbye Family (2020)

www.ingramcontent.com/pod-product-compliance
Lightning Source LLC
LaVergne TN
LVHW051918060526
838200LV00021B/388/J